JournEy HomE:
Serenity's Journey

ISBN: 978-1-967361-98-4 Paperback
ISBN: 978-1-967361-99-1 Ebook

Rev. date: 07/10/2025

JournEy HomE: Serenity's Journey

CORAL BARRETT

GLOSSARY

dhampir. Half vampire and half human.

falcon. A race not known to humans, with many types of magic users.

feeder. A source of blood, mainly humans.

pureblood. One hundred percent vampire or human.

shape-shifter. A being that can take on human form along with one or more other forms.

VHs. vampire hunters, a human or dhampir who hunts vampires.

VHS. Vampire Hunters Society, a group that hunts vampires.

CHARACTERS

Serenity – She has silver hair, silver eyes, and fair skin. She mainly wears a dark purple tank top, black leather jeans, black shoes, and a black trench coat.

Nightmare III – He has long black hair, purple eyes, and tan skin. He wears a black T-shirt, leather pants, a trench coat, and black leather boots.

Cloud – He has short blond hair, blue eyes, and tan skin. He has blue wings.

Dr. Clide – He has short blond hair. He wears a white coat, blue shirt, black tie, black pants, and black shoes.

Janine – She has green hair, green eyes, and tan skin. She wears a yellow dress and high heels. She will dress down and blend when needed.

Jonathan – He has silver and black hair, black eyes, and fair skin. He wears a long black and gold dress coat, dress pants, and a red shirt—the traditional attire for the royal family. When absolutely necessary, he will dress down to blend in. For instance, if working in a casino, he wears an orange top, black dress pants, and black dress shoes.

Scott – He has green hair silver highlights, green eyes, and tan skin. He is dressed in a long red and black dress coat and red and black dress pants—a traditional attire. But he normally wears a black and green vest, a grey T-shirt, back and green jeans, and black boots.

Konvict – He has green hair, silver eyes, and tan skin. He wears a painted blue and gold dress—a traditional attire.

Justin Hathaway – Nightmare III's grandfather on his mother's side.

Lillian Hathaway – Nightmare III's grandmother on his mother's side.

Roza – Serenity's old friend and personal maid. She has red hair, pale skin, and red eyes. She attends to Princess Serenity's every need.

Charles – Head of the royal guard in Capulet lands. He has light green hair and light blue eyes. He is a royal prince from another land. He gave up his title to serve as Princess Serenity's guard and to direct the rest of the guards. His full title is Prince Charles Grincory. He was the second prince in line back in his homeland.

PROLOGUE 1

Lord Capulet is the lord of Irshrose lands. He has silver and black hair, black eyes, and fair skin. He wears a long black and gold dress coat, dress pants, and a red shirt—the traditional attire for the royal family. Lady Jannie has green hair, green eyes, and tan skin. She wears traditional attire: a gold and red dress and gold dress shoes. They decided to take their youngest children on a family vacation to America to get away from Russia for a month and have some real family time. The children's names are Konvict, Jonathan, Serenity, and Scott. Konvict has green hair, silver eyes, and tan skin. He is dressed in a painted blue and gold dress got—a traditional attire. Scott has green hair with silver highlights. He is dressed in a long red and black dress coat and red and black dress pants—also traditional attire. Konvict and Scott are the only two biological children of Jonathan and Janine. Jonathan and Jannie wanted time with Serenity and Scott before the big royal ball that is to be hosted on Serenity's birthday to find her a suitor. She is the heir of her royal family. They will fly tonight, so they are now making final preparation for their vacation.

Serenity is hoping that she is going to get a chance to finally relax. She has been putting up with training day in and day out from her mother and royal tutors. She always felt as if she didn't fit in with most of her family. Serenity's only real connection was with her brother Jonathan. Her brothers Konvict and Scott bully her. Konvict is twelve years older than her, and Jonathan is eight years older than her. Serenity looks nothing like Jonathan, Jannie, Konvict, or Scott. But she looks a lot like her brother Jonathan. Jonathan and Serenity share no traits with Lord Capulet and Lady Jannie. Serenity is twenty-four years old, and her parents want her to take over the family land now. Serenity has no interest in running a family land that she suspects she is not a legitimate heir to. She hopes that this trip will allow her to put the voice that tells her otherwise at be at ease and reassure herself that she is the rightful heir in the family.

Serenity walks into her room. It has king size bed at the center, decorated with wolf blankets and pillows. She walks into the closet across from the bed. She makes sure she has packed what she needed in case of an emergency or when she has to flee America on short notice. The family decided to use one of their aliases. Every member of the royal family has to travel with a go-pack in case of emergencies overseas. Serenity can't wait to spend time in America away from her cage.

One of Serenity's private maids walks into her room.

"Excuse me, my princess. Can I give you a hand with anything?" asks Roza.

"Please draw me up a bath. I would like to take one before we leave," says Serenity.

"Yes, my princess," replies Roza, happy to help her princess.

Serenity is looking over the civilian clothes she has gathered over years form when she wanted to go out into the lands mostly unnoticed. Serenity picks out an outfit that her father would approve of. It was a pink tank top, blue jeans, a blue denim jacket, and a pair of blue sneakers. She decides not to choose her favorite outfit because her father would not approve of it. Her favorite outfit is black jeans, a purple tank top, a black leather jacket, and black sneakers. Serenity can't wait until they are more relaxed in America and able to wear what she would want over what her father approves of.

Serenity wishes her brother Jonathan could get the time off and join them on the family vacation to America. But his work is importunate to him and the survival of the family. He works on a Russian military base owned by their family head of the science department. Roza walks out of Serenity's private bathroom.

"My princess, your bath is ready," says Roza, happy to assist Serenity.

"Thank you, Roza," replies Serenity.

Serenity then walks from her bed where she was packing halfway across the room to the bathroom. She walks into the bathroom and undresses to take a nice relaxing bath before their departure. Serenity is thinking about everything she has been having dreams of in the past. But if they are true, then the life she knows is false. After thirty minutes, she gets out of the bathroom and returns to her bedroom to get dressed. She checks the clock next to her bed in a bath towel, and it reads 5:00 p.m.

Serenity wears her light blue dress, light blue high heels, and light blue dress coat that match. She decides not to push her luck and put on royal attire for the plane ride. It is early April, so she doesn't want to stand out with nothing covering her arms.

Her mother walks in right after she finished getting dressed.

"My daughter, we must be going," says Lady Jannie.

"Okay, I'm coming, Mother," says Serenity.

Jannie walks out of the room, not checking if his daughter is behind her or not. Serenity stops at her bedroom door and takes one last look around her bedroom. Serenity wishes she knew the truth about her royal family.

She doesn't linger on the thoughts. At this point, there is nothing she can do. After all, she is not allowed access to royal archives because her father considers it trivial. The woman in the family doesn't need to know the family history.

They are staying in their winter home which has one of their private airports. Lord Capulet is old-fashioned when it comes to his private property. He uses horse and buggy over a car.

PROLOGUE 2

Serenity, her bother Scott, her father Jonathan, and her mother Janine travel from Russia to America for a vacation away from their homelands. Serenity and her family never traveled outside Russia for vacation until now. Serenity and her family land in America from an incoming plane from Russia. They get off the plane in an orderly fashion, walking through the airport to baggage claim to get their suitcases. They walk outside to catch a cab to their hotel.

They wait outside the airport, standing in their traditional attire as royals from a foreign country to get a ride to their hotel. The cab pulls up, and the four of them ride in the same cab to the hotel, hungry and exhausted from a long flight from Russia to America. Once the cab stops in front of their hotel, they all get out and grab their luggage. It's late at night when finally get into the lobby of the hotel from their flight. The hotel they are staying at is not that far from the carnival that going on.

Scott has green hair with natural silver highlights, tan skin, and green eyes. He dresses in a green jacket with silver strips, green gloves, and green shorts with silver strips. He shares a room with Serenity, who has silver hair, silver eyes, and pale skin. She wears a light blue dress and light blue high heels.

Janine has long green hair and tan skin. She wears a yellow dress and yellow high heels and shares a room with Jonathan, who has silver and black hair, black eyes, and pale skin. He wears a royal male uniform in gold and royal blue colors. They look a lot different from normal families, but this will be their first time spending a lot of time around humans. For Serenity and Jonathan, they are a natural food source.

Scott and Serenity get a double bedroom, and Janine and Jonathan get a single bedroom. They are normally up at night, but they are going by human schedule while in America. They are trying very hard not to get caught being vampires and dhampirs.

It's early morning. Serenity and her family are getting ready for a fun-filled day at the carnival. Serenity dresses down in a pink T-shirt, blue jeans, and pink shoes. She ties her hair back to stay cool.

They are miles away from home. They leave their hotel at 10:00 a.m. and are due to return at 9:00 p.m.

At the carnival, Serenity and her family are having a blast, looking at exhibits, going on rides, and looking at the animals. But as it becomes dark, Serenity and her father can feel the tension of their hunger for blood.

They look around, and all they see are humans—their natural blood source. Serenity and her family all work to lure the prey into the dark parts of the carnival. Her father and her only take what they need to satisfy them. They erase their victim's memory and cover up bite marks so that no one sees them with the magic that Jonathan and Serenity possess. Scott and Janine stand guard to make sure no bystanders find out what going on—Scott at one end of the dark ally and Janine at the other end. When they are done, they walk back to their hotel. As soon as they walk in, they are met by the front desk clerk.

"Capulet family, please wait up. Your rooms were broken in to and destroyed," says the clerk.

"It's fine. We will collect stuff and pay for the damage cost to the hotel," says Jonathan.

"Okay," says the clerk before letting them go to their rooms to collect their belongings.

Once they reach their rooms, they pack what they could fit into one suitcase: the priority items, including their emergency funds and aliases, along with whatever weapons and clothes they can fit in it. After they all got packed, they leave the hotel and catch a cab to the airport. Once there, Serenity uses her magic to make sure her mother's and brother's luggage made it past security.

They made a pack as a family that no matter what happens, no one will return home except Serenity. Then she will go after the rest of the family and reunite everyone.

They all buy tickets for separate flights from America to their chosen destinations. Serenity chooses Scotland, Scott chooses Japan, and Janine and Jonathan choose China. If for any reason a vampire hunter catches one of them, they wouldn't get caught all at the same time.

Serenity is waiting for her flight out of America all alone and anxious.

PART 1

Vampire Hunter Trouble

CHAPTER 1

Serenity enters Scotland in the early morning from an incoming airplane from America. Serenity starts walking around the city to find a hotel to stay in while in Scotland. While walking through the empty streets with tall buildings to find the perfect hotel, she finds a high-class hotel and walks inside to get a room. She decides to get the best room available for a long-term stay. Serenity walks over to the front desk clerk to try and reserve a room.

"Miss, can I help you?" asks the front desk clerk dressed in a suit.

"I would like a room, please. I'm visiting for a while before returning home," says Serenity.

"Okay, but the only room currently available for a long-term stay is the penthouse suite," says the clerk.

"I'll take it," says Serenity then pays for it in advance.

The clerk hands Serenity the key to the penthouse suite. She then walks over to the elevator and takes it up to her penthouse suite. She walks into the penthouse suite, surprised to see it laid out like a house. It has a kitchen on the left and a living room on the right, off the foyer. After walking the hall, she finds an office on the left and a bathroom and laundry on right. She has to go upstairs to get to the bedrooms. Once upstairs, Serenity checks out the four bedrooms to see which one she likes the best.

Once she chooses the bedroom she likes, Serenity goes inside and quickly unpacks her suitcase. She then changes into her tank top andbed shorts. She then crawls into bed and goes to sleep.

Serenity wakes up later that night. She gets dressed to go out. She puts on a pair of blue jeans and a green tank top. She walks out of her bedroom, down the stairs, and out the penthouse door. She takes the elevator downstairs and leaves the hotel for a night stroll.

While walking, Serenity spots a very old unused road and decides she wants to check it out. It's late and right around midnight. The moon is full and high in the sky. There is no one out and about.

All of a sudden, a carriage appears, and a gentleman steps out of it. The carriage is all-black with windows. It has two black vampiric horses with red eyes, pulling the carriage.

The gentleman has black hair that goes half way down his back, purple eyes, and tan skin. He is wearing skin-tight black leather pants. He also has a black leather jacket with all different sizes of studs on it. Serenity can see what he is wearing because of the moonlight and clear sky, in addition to her vampiric vision.

"Miss, you shouldn't be out here," says the gentleman.

"Why, is it a crime to wander around here at night?" asks Serenity.

"No, it's not. What is your name, if I may inquire?" asks the gentleman.

"It's Lilly. Or at least that's what I go by," says Serenity.

"No, I want your real name, not what people call you by," he says.

"Okay, it's Serenity, and may I inquire about yours?" asks Serenity.

"No, you can't have mine yet, Serenity, dear. I'll tell you when the time is right. I must go," says the gentleman.

"But, sir, I must get to know you," says Serenity.

"Serenity, not now. I'll send my carriage here tomorrow at midnight sharp. Be here if you truly want to get to know me. Only then will you get my name," says the gentleman.

She starts walking back to her hotel, thinking about the sexy, tan gentle man she met, unaware he is following her back. Serenity walks through the hotel doors and asks for her room key, then she took the elevator up to her room. When she gets inside, she walks to her room, then into the bathroom attached to her room, and takes a long shower with him on her mind. It is three in the morning when she finally gets to bed. Serenity starts dreaming about him.

He is watching her sleep for a while in the shadows of her room. Then just before dawn, he teleports outside, rides his carriage back to his family's secondary castle, and goes to bed. He has fallen in love with this mysterious unknown commoner. He has never felt this way before .

CHAPTER 2

Serenity wakes up at 4:00 p.m. and leaves her hotel room to go out to her favorite clothing store and find something a little more suitable to wear for the meeting with the mysterious man she met last night. When Serenity gets there, she quickly finds a good pair of jeans and a nice top. The jeans are faded; they go from black to gray. The tank top she picks is red fading into pink, with a v-cut in the front. She pays $60 for both of them. It's now 5:00 p.m., and Serenity walks back to her hotel to get cleaned up and ready for tonight. She is not one bit scared of what this pale man will do to her.

Serenity rides the elevator back up to her penthouse suite. She then walks upstairs to the room that she is staying in. Serenity walks over to her bed and lays down her clothes before walking into the bathroom and showering to prepare for her meeting with the gentle man she met the night before.

Serenity decides to leave her hotel at 9:00 p.m. so that she can walk around a bit before meeting the carriage at midnight. But while she is walking around the city, she encounters trouble. A young man grabs her and throws her over his shoulder. He carries her to the abandoned apartment building on the other side of the city away from where she needs to be. It is where he likes to squat. She starts struggling to get away. He forces her down. Serenity tries screaming for help. She is trying to act human but is not. Serenity is still struggling until she finally catches him off guard, and then she throws him aside and runs away from the abandoned apartment building.

It's almost midnight, and she is running to the spot where she is supposed to meet the carriage. Her brand-new clothes are dirty from the abandoned apartment building. Her heart is racing from adrenaline from the attack and experience in the apartment building. She reaches the meeting spot right as the church bells ring at midnight.

The carriage appears in front of her. She gets in, feeling exhausted and hungry. She is a pureblood vampire. She falls asleep right away, tired from using too much of her powers.

When the carriage comes to a stop, the master of the horses comes outside the carriage. He opens the carriage doors to find Serenity sound asleep. He picks her up and carries her to his room. When he gets inside his room, Nightmare III gently lays her down on the bed. He lays down next to her and holds her close to him. He doesn't know she is his perfect match since they are both purebloods.

She wakes up to find herself in his arms.

"Umm, sir, why are you holding me instead of me being in the carriage? Where am I?" asks Serenity.

"You're in my family's secondary castle in Scotland, Serenity dear. I wanted you close to me and don't want you to leave me for someone else," says the man.

"Why me out of all the girls in Scotland?" asks Serenity.

"I love you with all my heart, Serenity," says the man.

"Sorry, I can't love someone I don't know," says Serenity.

"Okay, Serenity, you win," says the man.

"What is your name and could you tell me about yourself? In return, I'll tell you about me," says Serenity.

"My name is Nightmare Shadow Dragon III. What would you like to know about me, my dear?" says Nightmare III.

"I want to know everything about you," says Serenity.

"Okay, where do we start?" asks Nightmare III.

"At the beginning, please," asks Serenity.

CHAPTER 3

"I was born in Japan's Firelands with my two sisters, Coalwind and Jade. We always come here to Scotland every summer vacation to spend time with our grandparents. We had fun while we were spending time with our grandparents who live here in Scotland. We did everything from ballroom dancing to swimming in rivers. We always got to meet many people. We even had summertime friends. But it all had to eventually come to an end, and we all grow up. Most of our friends are married and have families of their own," says Nightmare III.

He continues, "I didn't find my true love like they did until I met you. I was wondering if you could give me a chance at loving you. I need a lover, a friend, and someone I can just depend on. I would be happy if you could meet my grandparents and the rest of my family sometime. I would like to eventually marry you and have a family of our own. I don't want to be alone ever again in this cruel cold-hearted world. Everyone here is unpredictable and harsh—here in Scotland and back in Japan."

"Okay, Nightmare III, we will see what happens. Now it's my turn to tell you my story," says Serenity.

"Okay, go ahead, Serenity dear. I'm listening," says Nightmare III.

CHAPTER 4

"I came here from America because our hotel rooms were broken into. They were destroyed, and we can't return home right away, so I choose to come here to Scotland. My family is actually from Russia. I have a mother named Janine and a father named Jonathan. My brother who went on vacation with us is named Scott. While we were on our vacation, something went wrong during our stay at the hotel, so we all had to separate and go to different countries. I love my family and miss them a lot. Last night was my first night outside my hotel. I had been here in Scotland for a little over a week now," narrates Serenity.

She continues, "My family's lands are unique, filled with exotic flowers and pure and clear waters. It's nice there all year around. My family is very close. My mother and father love to spoil me, and my brother tries to act older and more responsible. He tries to protect me, keep me safe, and watches over me. People in America don't like people different from them. So we had humans and dhampirs attacking us for that reason."

She goes on, "We are royals. My father and I are vampires, and my mother and brother are dhampirs. My family can live for many years. We used to live on a planet of our own, but it died after people brought destruction with their filthy machines. We had to relocate somewhere on Earth, so we went to Russia. Now we have vampire hunters after us for standing out while visiting America. We are all trying to not get caught, and if someone does get caught, it won't be all of us at once. There may come a time when I'll have to leave because I'm being chased by vampire hunters. I don't wish to get you involved with my family troubles."

"If I do leave, go to Russia where my family lives and wait for me there. I like you a lot. I do wish that someday we can be together and that I won't have to ever leave your side again. I would to like meet your family someday, as well as for you to meet my family. I guess you could say I have fallen for you. I like your beautiful black long hair, purple eyes, and your muscular body. That's how I ended up here in Scotland. I'm really glad I came here out of all my other choices on the globe," says Serenity.

CHAPTER 5

It's late morning when Serenity and Nightmare III went to sleep the same way he was holding her after he took her out of the carriage earlier that morning. The servants are cleaning the castle and preparing the master's and the young lady's meal when they got up and out of bed. While they sleep, he holds her as close to him as possible. Her scent is of a wild flower. He gets lost in her scent and falls asleep instead of watching her sleep in his arms.

When they awaken, they walk through winding hallways to the dining hall to have food that was prepared while they were asleep. The hallways are lined with gems. The rims on board are painted navy blue, his Grandfather Justin's favorite color. The dining hall is beautiful. It's full of life and color. It has chandeliers hanging from the ceiling. The walls are painted gold with black trim and gems on board. They eat in silence, then walk back to Nightmare III's bedroom. They walk into the connecting bathroom to shower.

The castle is filled with many rooms, but Serenity chooses to go into a master bath that is connected to Nightmare III's room. She gets undressed and steps into the shower. Nightmare goes into the bathroom after her, undresses, and joins her.

"Nightmare, why are you in here with me?" asks Serenity.

"I couldn't help myself. You're so sexy, I just wanted to shower with you," says Nightmare III.

"Fine, I don't care. Just don't touch," says Serenity.

"Okay, I can wait until later to get you," says Nightmare III.

They get out of the shower and walk back into the room to get dressed, but with Serenity still wrapped in a towel, Nightmare III pins her to the bed.

"Nightmare, why are you pinning me down?" asks Serenity.

"Because I'm horny. I want sex—a child with you and you forever," says Nightmare III.

"Nightmare, it will have to wait until I'm not being hunted, sorry," says Serenity.

"Okay, I'll wait even if I have to wait forever," says Nightmare III.

He lets her up, and they both get dressed. He is going to take her to meet his grandparents, even if this may not last forever like they want it to. She walks next to him in silence, not knowing what to say. She breaks his heart as she reminds him that she is not here on a vacation but as a hideout from VHs who are still after her.

They finally get to his grandparents' place after walking across the courtyard. He doesn't know how to tell them the one he loves is in trouble with hunters. He knocks on the door and his grandmother answers.

"Grandson, come on in and bring the lovely girl in too," says Lillian.

"Grandson, why did you bring this girl with you tonight?" asks his grandfather, Justin.

"Grandfather, she is the one I want as my mate, but there are some complications," says Nightmare III.

"What type of complications, Grandson?" asks his grandfather, Justin.

"She has vampire hunters after her, Grandfather, and she was separated from her family. Her name is Serenity," says Nightmare III.

"Serenity, what can you do for our grandson and why?" asks Justin.

"Anything—even kids but after I'm out of trouble so that I don't endanger the pregnancy," says Serenity.

"Okay, Serenity, we approve of you, but we want to meet your family," says Justin.

"You will when it's safe," says Serenity.

Nightmare III takes Serenity into a private room to rest. Serenity lies down next to Nightmare III. All Serenity wants is a peaceful life with the vampire she wants as her mate, which she can't have until she gets rid of her pursuers.

CHAPTER 6

When she wakes up, Nightmare III is still fast asleep. Serenity leaves the room. She notices a painting on the wall as she steps out into the hallway. She stares at it and notices it was a family portrait. It has a tall man dressed in a traditional Japanese kimono. He has short black hair, purple eyes, and tan skin. There is also a woman in a traditional Japanese kimono. She has pale blond hair, white eyes, and tan skin. The first son standing next to lord has black and blond hair, one white eye and one black eye, and tan skin. The first daughter standing next to the woman has jade green eyes and hair and tan skin. She is also dressed in traditional Japanese kimono. The second son has long black hair, purple eyes, and tan skin. He dresses in traditional Japanese kimono. The second daughter has black hair, gold eyes, and tan skin. She is dressed in traditional kimono.

Serenity walks down the hall to the room on the left. She goes into the first room she finds. When she walks in, she finds walls upon walls of books. The shelves reach from floor to ceiling with many levels. She doesn't know where to begin to look for a book to read.

She starts on the first level of the library, and she finds a book she loves to read. She picks up the book, sits in a chair, and begins to read. While she is in the middle of reading, she hears Nightmare III's frantic voice, looking for her. She marks her place and takes the book with her to go meet up with him.

When she gets down from the top of the library, she cannot hear his voice anymore. So she keeps wandering the castle in hopes of running into Nightmare III. When she gets to a creepy part of the castle, she goes to explore it. She gets lost while exploring and forgets that she needs to meet up with Nightmare III.

She goes into a room with a sign on it saying, "Keep Out." She sees a feeder—what she considers food. Serenity can't contain herself around the feeders. She hasn't eaten in a few days so she feeds off one. The feeder was happy when Serenity gets done.

Serenity leaves the room and is finally found by Nightmare III. He walks her back to his room. When they get there, he wasn't angry with her. It is only natural that she feeds. If the humans know, they would freak out about the truth of what Nightmare III and she are. So they can't feed around the humans or let them know about the secret of their true form.

After about an hour or so, Serenity falls back to sleep. It is still day and natural for her to sleep at this hour. Nightmare III holds her close, wanting her in the safest place in the castle. When she wakes up in his arms, she starts cuddling him. Serenity is in love with him, but it can't last forever. She gets up to leave him behind while he is asleep just to keep him out of harm's way. Serenity leaves the castle and starts walking through a labyrinth garden to leave the grounds. She is trying to get back to her hotel in case vampire hunters come after her.

CHAPTER 7

As Serenity is walking back to her hotel, she senses that the VHs have arrived in Scotland. She takes a detour, heading for the other side of the country. Serenity finds a park with trails running behind it and takes a trail to throw off her pursuers. She finds people on the trail, and she strikes up a conversation with them, acting normally to throw off any hunters who may be on the trail as well.

They are walking together on the trail, and after a while, they are the only ones left. It is amusing that the humans think she is one of them—just one of them but with a birth defect, giving her hair, eyes, and skin a strange color. When she gets alone with the humans, she puts a sleeping spell on them. She takes some blood and erases their memory of her ever talking to them. But they are left with bite marks on the neck. She uses magic to cover up the bite marks she left behind.

She walks to the bar in town to stall going back to the hotel, but she doesn't plan to drink. She would rather shoot pool.

She gets into the bar easily, and she goes to the pool table and challenges anyone to play her if they dare. A biker named Mad Dog takes her challenge, thinking she is all talk and no game. Mad Dog has dirty blond hair, blue eyes, and tan skin. He is wearing a leather vest, leather jeans, and leather boots. She gives him the first shot. He puts two stripe balls in a pocket at once but then misses on his next shot.

Serenity shoots one in after another until she gets all the solids and the eight ball in the pockets. Game over. She turns and leaves. Mad dog follows her outside. When she gets outside, Mad Dog grabs her arm, angry that he lost to a female. She shoves him away and calls him a sore loser. She leaves him on the ground and heads back to her hotel.

Meanwhile, back at Nightmare III's family's secondary castle, he is getting ready to wake up.

CHAPTER 8

Nightmare wakes up to find a letter addressed to him, and Serenity is missing. He opens the letter to read it.

Dear Nightmare III,

Thanks for everything, but I must go due to trouble. Do not come after me and don't worry. I'm capable of throwing them off my trail and caring for myself. Please meet me in Russia in the Irshrose lands.

Sincerely,
Serenity Irshrose Capulet

Nightmare goes to his grandparent's house to tell them that he is going after his love to try to save her from her pursuers. His grandfather answers the door, asking what is wrong.

"I can't explain right now. I just have to go after Serenity," says Nightmare III.

Nightmare III runs back to the castle to get his carriage, knowing he is risking it all to find Serenity and keep her safe. He doesn't care about the price it might cost him to get her home safe and sound. He loves her more than anything in the world.

Back in town Serenity, is at her hotel.

CHAPTER 9

Serenity gets back to the hotel and asks for a room key from the night clerk.

"I'm sorry, but unfortunately, your room was raided, and some of your belongings were destroyed," says the night clerk.

Serenity says she'll pay the damage fees later, but she must go now. She rushes to her room to see what is missing, and she finds a letter on the stand next to the bed. It says:

Ms. Serenity,

If you wish to see this hotel unharmed, meet us in the open field tonight at 9:00 p.m., or else everyone in the hotel will be blown up.

It is already 8:45 p.m. Serenity easily picks up their scent from far away. She runs through the wood to find and kill these vampire hunters for threatening her and endangering others. She travels through the trees so that she can stay off the ground and avoid their traps.

She spots the vampire hunters up ahead. She studies the VHs very closely—every move. She looks for an opening, a way to get out of this alive and save those at the hotel who are innocent bystanders. Serenity counts how many VHs there are to figure out the best way to take them down. She studies them long and hard. Serenity learns that their leader, Jack, has a weak spot for vampires because he is part one. She gets as close as she can without getting caught. From a fresh cut on her hand, she lets the blood drip to the ground from a tree branch instead of drinking her own blood.

Jack tells his men to be on guard because he hears dripping blood coming from a short distance and doesn't know what it is that is injured.

CHAPTER 10

Serenity jumps down to attack the VHs. They are shocked that she is up that high. Jack fires a gun. Although the bullet wounds her, it does not stop her from attacking them back. Serenity starts to use a whip on them, but someone gets in between them and her. She doesn't dare to harm the man. She doesn't recognize him.

She senses that he is another vampire, but his face is covered in hopes that she would kill him along with the vampire hunters. Serenity finds it difficult to get around this vampire to kill her enemies, so she lets out her secret weapon to kill them all. After everyone falls to the ground, she begins to look through the battlefield for the detonator. She can't find it anywhere, but all of a sudden, she hears someone trying to breathe. She goes to find out if anyone is still alive. She walks through the dead bodies and blood. She follows the sound, and as she gets closer, she sees the masked vampire. She goes to take the mask off him.

"No, let me die. Find what you were looking for on the battlefield."

She feels his life slipping away, and she is unsure what to do.

Even if Serenity heals him, he may still die. So she heals him and uses her magic to take the blood of her enemies to save this vampire's life. Then she continues to search for the detonator. Serenity finally finds a dead man holding it. She takes the detonator and defuses it, then leaves to return to the hotel—tired, weak, and vulnerable to attacks. Serenity doesn't want to leave Scotland quite yet without clearing things up with Nightmare III.

It's close to dawn now. It is time for Serenity to go to bed, but she still has a long walk back to her hotel. She doesn't know someone is waiting for her back in her room.

CHAPTER 11

She walks through the woods toward her hotel when she spots three humans walking along, drunk and swaying. She puts them out with magic and then takes what she needs from each without killing them. She covers the mark on their neck so that others won't know that they were bitten by a vampire.

She continues walking through the woods to get back before sunrise. The thought of that vampire interfering and risking death weighs heavily on her mind. She thinks it is strange that the vampire helped her. It reminds her of what Nightmare III would do for her. But she knows she had to do what she did to save the lives of the people at the hotel.

Serenity sees the sun starting to come over the horizon. She is still too far away to make it back to the hotel before the sun comes up. Serenity doesn't know that a man is waiting for her back in her hotel room. She is too weak to rush back to the hotel after saving that vampire's life. She sees the hotel in sight, and the sun is up now, weakening her further.

She walks into her hotel, only being gone all night, and asks for her room key. The day clerk thinks it odd to see Serenity still up.

"Ms. Capulet, a guest is waiting for you outside your penthouse suite," says the day clerk.

"Thank you for informing me," says Serenity.

Serenity goes to her room to find out who is her visitor since Nightmare III is the only one who knows where she is staying. She finds one of her enemies who survived the battle and is standing there before her. She takes a step toward him.

"I come in peace, and there is something you should know before attacking and killing me for attacking you on the battlefield," says the man.

"Speak now before I attack you and kill you for your insolence in confronting me alone after trying to kill me," says Serenity.

"I came here to apologize for attacking you. I never wanted to hurt you, Princess Serenity, but I had no choice if I wanted to survive. My name is Cloud. I'm a friend of your family. If there is any way at all that I can make it up to you, name it, and I'll be more than happy to serve you as you wish. I'm a fellow demon, a falcon to be specific," says Cloud.

"Okay, Cloud, I'll accept your apology. I need a bodyguard while I rest. I'm tired and want to get some sleep. I had a long day, so wait here while I go bathe. Don't attack any other demon, especially if one named Nightmare III comes here. He is a dear friend of mine and a possible lover," says Serenity.

"Yes, Princess Serenity, I understand perfectly clear," says Cloud.

Serenity walks upstairs to her bedroom, goes to the bathroom, and starts the water, thinking about how nice it would be to bathe or shower with Nightmare III. She is falling in love with the vampire who saved her life more than once in many different ways. While she is washing up, she falls asleep in the tub, enjoying the warm water running down her body and the peace and quietness of the hotel room. Serenity needs the rest after the long day out fighting the vampire hunters.

She wakes up after the water turns cold, then she gets out of the shower and goes back into her room. She puts on her bedclothes then gets into bed and starts reading a book, but she soon falls asleep with the book on her chest. She starts dreaming about having Nightmare III as the one she loves forever and ever. Serenity doesn't realize how much she loves him. She also doesn't know how much she can't live without him, and the only thing on her mind is him.

CHAPTER 12

It's just after sunset, and someone is knocking on Serenity's hotel room door. Cloud, who is guarding Serenity but staying downstairs in the penthouse, gets up and answers the door to find out who is at the door since Serenity wasn't expecting a guest. He was surprised to see it was a vampire at the door.

"Please move and leave," asks the vampire.

"No, my name is Cloud, and I'm her protector, and she mustn't be disturbed," says Cloud.

"Could you just move to the side? My name is Nightmare III, and nothing will stop me from getting to her," says Nightmare III.

"Fine, but if you hurt her, I'll personally kill you and make sure you remain dead. Do we have an understanding, Vampire?" asks Cloud.

"Yes, but it won't be easy to kill me, Cloud. I don't go down without a fight," says Nightmare III.

"We will see, Nightmare III, if it comes down to it. For now, you are fine. Just don't get on my bad side, or I'll make your life a living hell until you die. And trust me, I don't want to hurt Princess Serenity," says Cloud.

CHAPTER 13

Serenity is surprised to see Nightmare III walk into her hotel room knowing Cloud is guarding it.

"Nightmare III, what are you doing here in my hotel room?" asks Serenity.

"I need us to talk alone please, if possible," asks Nightmare III.

"Okay, Nightmare III, it can be done," says Serenity.

Serenity turns to Cloud and speaks.

"Cloud, please give Nightmare III and me a minute and wait outside the room," asks Serenity.

"Yes, Princess," says Cloud.

Serenity leads Nightmare III to her private room in the penthouse suite.

"Nightmare III, what did you want to talk about now that we are alone?" asks Serenity.

"Serenity, I want to know if you love me and will marry me," asks Nightmare III.

"Nightmare, I can't answer your questions right now," says Serenity.

"Why not, Serenity? We spent a lot of time together, and I know you're not afraid of me. What makes it so hard on you?" asks Nightmare III.

"I have my family to worry about, and I don't want to drag you into this war with the vampire hunters. You're a good man," says Serenity.

"Serenity it is too late. I'm already involved," says Nightmare III.

"How are you already involved?" asks Serenity.

"I am the vampire you almost killed and then saved. I dressed up like that so you wouldn't recognize me," says Nightmare III.

"Why? You could have died and not come back!" asks Serenity.

"That was a chance I needed to take, Serenity. I love you, and I don't want you to die. I don't care what happens to me as long as you live," says Nightmare III.

"I don't love you and never will, so stop putting yourself in harm's way because of me," says Serenity.

"Never, Serenity. Nothing you say will change what I do," says Nightmare III.

He pushes her down on the bed.

"Nightmare III, what are you thinking!" asks Serenity.

"Strip for me, Serenity," says Nightmare III.

"What, are you crazy?" asks Serenity.

"No, I'm dead serious. Strip for me, or I'll strip the both of us," says Nightmare III.

"If you want sex, you will have to undress me yourself with me fighting you," says Serenity.

"Fine, I will, Serenity, with pleasure doing so," says Nightmare III.

"What are you going do to me?" asks Serenity.

"Things your pretty little head shouldn't worry about," says Nightmare III.

"Will you attempt to get me pregnant? And if you get me pregnant, you will be sorry after meeting my father," says Serenity.

"I'm not afraid because we need to marry any female we get pregnant," says Nightmare III.

"Nightmare III, I'm not a puppet you can use and command," says Serenity.

"I know. I love you, and I can read it in your eyes that you love me too," says Nightmare III.

"I can't love anyone I just met," says Serenity.

Exhausted from the day and the discussion, Serenity and Nightmare III lay down to get some sleep.

CHAPTER 14

It is early morning and Serenity is leaving her hotel room to go to the library to look up information. When she gets there, she spots a man dressed all in black, standing in the doorway.

"Sir, can I please get through?" asks Serenity.

"Only if I see your ID," says the man in black.

Serenity shows the man her ID, and he allows her to pass. She goes into a seldom-used section of the library and finds the books she is looking for. The books are about the most effective way to kill most vampire hunters at once. She starts reading one of her books and spots a man following her. She stands up and heads to the checkout counter. The man in black steps in Serenity's direction. Other men, also in black, follow his lead. She runs out of the library, but the men follow her. Serenity leads them to an unpopulated area to talk to them, even knowing it may end up in a fight. She stops quickly and throws the books away from her.

"What do you want with me?" asks Serenity.

"We are after you, you ungrateful vampires. You're associating with humans and killing them," says the leader.

"I'm not killing them but am feeding off them and erasing their memory of the event," says Serenity.

"Why do you bother to try to explain yourself to us?" says the leader.

"Because I don't want a fight, but I will if it comes down to that," says Serenity.

Serenity is guarded, realizing the men in black are really VHs.

CHAPTER 15

The vampire hunters start to attack Serenity. A strange man in black with a cape starts to attack her pursuers. Serenity tries to avoid injury from the vampire hunters who are after her, but with the strange man, it is harder to do so. They are also using weapons that don't harm humans but will kill or do serious damage to vampires and other demons easily. She needs to make a difficult decision that involves life or death.

It starts to rain down where they are fighting. One of the VHs cuts her. That is when Serenity knew she now has no choice but to kill these vampire hunters. Serenity starts fighting the vampire hunters using her whip and takes out as many as she can, being outnumbered. As she is battling them, she manages to kill most of them before she passes out from blood loss.

CHAPTER 16

Nightmare III is worried. It has been several hours since Serenity left to go to the library. It is dark and dangerous outside. He decides that it is too dangerous for a female to be alone outside in this place. Nightmare III decides to go to the library to see if Serenity is still there.

"Sir, can I help you with something?" asks the woman at the checkout counter.

"Yes, have you seen a female who is from a foreign country in here at all today?" asks Nightmare III.

"Why, yes, she ran with books," says the woman.

"Was anyone chasing her?" asks Nightmare III.

"Yes, there were men in black," answers the woman.

"Damn, that girl. She can get into a lot of trouble," says Nightmare III.

Nightmare III leaves the library in a panic, needing to find Serenity. He needs to make sure Serenity is okay and safe.

CHAPTER 17

The remaining men take Serenity back to their hideout. When Serenity finally comes around, she finds that she is chained down, and the leader is next to her.

"Miss, what is your name?" asks Leader Jack.

"Why should I tell a scum bag like you?" asks Serenity.

"Because either way, I will do as I please with you," says Jack.

"Do it. I'm not scared of you," says Serenity.

"Okay, we will find out about that right now," says Jack.

He cuts Serenity's clothes off her body, with her still chained down to the bed. He makes sure all the loose pieces of clothes are moved away from her body and off the bed, then he undresses himself. He gets on top of her.

She screams from the pain from it. She never had sex before, but part of her likes it. She hates herself for being clumsy after a hard fight.

CHAPTER 18

Nightmare III hears screaming from far away. He rushes toward the sound, unsure of what to expect. But he knows that no matter what, he can't let Serenity die so far away from home, knowing that her family will miss their daughter and family land's princess. It takes him thirty minutes to find the hidden cottage where screams are coming from. Nightmare III finds her after rushing inside the cottage, searching for her. Even though the screaming stopped, it doesn't mean that she is dead.

Nightmare III follows the blood trail that Serenity left as she was carried back. Nightmare III sees Serenity chained down to the bed. He rushes to her side. She opens her eyes and sees him, and she tries to get away from him, scared and confused over what's going on.

"You will be safe from now on. I won't let anything happen to you ever again," says Nightmare III.

She looks at him with pleading eyes. She is cut up pretty badly and is in a lot of pain from the beating she took from the fight the night before. Nightmare III gets the chains off her and wraps her in his cape. He heads toward the door with her in his arms.

CHAPTER 19

The man in black walks into the cottage.

"You men, get out of my way or die. I'm a vampire, and unlike this girl, I will have no problem taking you out," says Nightmare III.

"Prove it, lay her down, and fight us. If you win, you two can walk out of here alive," says one of the vampire hunters.

"Fine, since none of you will be alive when I'm done with you," says Nightmare III.

He lays Serenity down on the couch. Nightmare III takes out his hidden weapon and charges at all the men in the room, slicing through one by one until they all lay dead on the floor, except for the leader who sneaked out like a coward while the men were being slaughtered like cattle.

After Nightmare III is done, he picks up Serenity and leaves. Serenity is too tired to notice what is going on. Nightmare III is worried about her condition. Nightmare III starts walking back toward the city to take Serenity to an emergency room.

CHAPTER 20

Nightmare brings Serenity into the hospital emergency room. He is carrying her in his arms through the emergency doors. The nurses rush toward them as they enter. Nightmare III takes a deep breath to talk to them.

"I need you to help her. She was badly injured. I found her undressed, so I wrapped her in my cape. If possible don't cut it up. I'll need it," says Nightmare III.

"Yes, sir," says one of the nurses.

"Do you know if she has family here to contact or notify if anything goes wrong?"

"No. I'll give you my number. I'm closest to her right now. Her family doesn't live here, and we don't know where they are located at the present."

"Okay, sir. Please wait in the waiting room. We will have that cape on her washed for you. We may need to use it for DNA and get the police involved. She looks like she has been sexually attacked too," says the nurse.

"Fine, do your job, but please keep her alive. I'll cooperate in any way I can. See that she is well," says Nightmare III.

"We'll do our best, of course, but most of it depends on her own will to live," says the nurse.

CHAPTER 21

After about five hours of stabilizing Serenity and disinfecting the wounds, the doctors stitch them and wheel her to ICU for recovery and rest. But first they need to do a rape kit on her while she is still asleep. The doctor goes to talk to Nightmare III. The doctor has blond hair blue eyes, and tan skin. He wears a white doctor coat, blue shirt, black tie, black dress pants, and black dress shoes.

"Doctor, how is she, and can I help you with anything?" asks Nightmare III.

"I need your DNA to rule you out as the one who attacked her," says the doctor.

"Okay, doctor, you can, but I can guarantee that you're pointing fingers at the wrong man," says Nightmare III.

"If that is true, you can see her in twenty minutes," says the doctor.

"Do what you need to do so I can be near her. She is my whole world," says Nightmare III.

A half-hour later, the doctor comes out and gives Nightmare III the clearance to go see Serenity. He sits down next to her and holds her hands to try to let Serenity know she is not alone. He is not sure if she can even tell he is in the room. So he just waits, sitting beside her, hoping she will come around and hoping she is only asleep because it is still daylight.

CHAPTER 22

Serenity is coming around after surgery, but she isn't out of the woods yet.

Nightmare III is still sitting at her bedside. Serenity looks around, unaware that she has been brought to the hospital. Nightmare III notices that she is starting to panic.

"Relax, Serenity, you're safe. I won't let anyone hurt you in the hospital," says Nightmare III.

"Nightmare, can we leave, please? I hate hospitals. They have white rooms," says Serenity.

Nightmare III picks up that something has happened to her I'm white rooms.

"Serenity, what happened to you in the white rooms before now?" asks Nightmare III.

She just keeps quiet from the painful memories.

"Serenity, please tell me. I want to help in any way possible," says Nightmare III.

The doctor comes into the room to see if Serenity is awake yet. He has blond hair, blue eyes, and tan skin. He wears a white doctor's coat, a blue dress shirt, black tie, black dress pants, and black dress shoes. Nightmare III gets up and walks over to the doctor.

"Dr. Clide, please take off your white coat," asks Nightmare III.

"As you wish," says Dr. Clide.

Dr. Clide takes off his white coat and hangs it by the door so that he doesn't scare his patient when he approaches her. He gets next to her bed side and checks her charts real quick before speaking to her.

"Serenity, my name is Dr. Clide. What's the matter, sugar?" inquires Dr. Clide.

"I want out of here. I hate white rooms or anything white that has something to do with a hospital," says Serenity.

"Why?" asks Dr. Clide.

"Because people kept me in white rooms with white hospital stuff," says Serenity.

"Do you know who these people are?" asks Dr. Clide.

"No, but they like hurting me," says Serenity.

"Calm down. The bad people can't hurt you here," says Dr. Clide.

"I don't care. I'm scared being here," says Serenity.

"Okay, sugar. Let me talk to my boss and see what I can do for you," says Dr. Clide.

Dr. Clide walks to the door and picks his coat up off the hanger before leaving the room to go and try to make arrangements for treating Serenity at home.

CHAPTER 23

Dr. Clide walks down the hall to his boss's room and knocks on the door of his boss's office. His boss answers the door and lets Dr. Clide in the office. His boss has short brown hair, green eyes, and tan skin. He dresses in a white doctor's coat, red dress shirt, black tie, black dress pants, and black dress shoes. His boss gestures for him to have seat. He can tell Dr. Clide came to talk. After they are both seated at the desk, his boss starts the conversation.

"What can I do for you tonight?" asks his boss.

"I need special consideration. I would like to take a patient home and work with her there. She is terrified of being here," says Dr. Clide.

"Why?" his boss inquires.

"Because of personal reasons that are scaring her around white rooms and hospital coats. I would like to see her recover without freaking out," says Dr. Clide.

"Okay, but it stays between us only. Take her out after most of everyone leaves. I'll tell security to shut down the cameras for an hour, from 9 to 10, so that you can get her out. I'll let the head doctor and nurse know as well and the reason for it," says his boss, agreeing to have her treated outside the hospital.

"Thank you, Boss," says Dr. Clide.

Dr. Clide gets up, leaves his boss's office, and heads back to speak with Serenity about the plan. It is about 6:30 p.m., and it is time for Dr. Clide to take a break. He is working until 8:30 p.m.

CHAPTER 24

Serenity falls back to sleep with Nightmare III in the room. She is tired from the surgery earlier that day. Nightmare III stays at her bedside, worried to death about her. He wants her to be safe and get the best care.

Dr. Clide walks back down the hallway he came from before returning to Serenity's hospital room. He can tell Serenity is resting because the room lights are off, and the only lights on are the hallway lights. The doctor motions to Nightmare III, hoping that Nightmare III understands that he wants to speak with him in the hallway.

Nightmare looks from Serenity and back to Dr. Clide. He is concerned for her best interest. He nods, and they step into the hall to talk.

"Dr. Clide, what are you planning for Serenity?" asks Nightmare III.

"Nothing that will harm her. Just have her up and ready to leave here by 9:00 p.m. She is coming to my house after it quiets down. It will help her get better. She won't have to be in a white room or around white doctor's coats. I can tell that bright lights and rooms are making her aggravated and that someone like her shouldn't be exposed to so many people in her condition," says Dr. Clide.

Nightmare III agrees to have her ready a little before 9:00 p.m. Serenity is weak but stable in the recovery room. She is strong enough to walk but doesn't dare to.

"Nightmare III, what are you doing?" asks Serenity.

"I'm getting your clothes. We need to get you dressed and ready to leave," says Nightmare III.

"Why, Nightmare III? What is going on?" asks Serenity.

"The doctor going to care for you outside of the hospital room, back at his house," says Nightmare III.

"That's fine as long as the doctors in white stay away," says Serenity.

"There won't be anyone but Dr. Clide. It will be safe and quiet just the way you like it," says Nightmare III.

Serenity is happy that she will be leaving here soon. It is a few minutes before 9:00 p.m., and Dr. Clide walks into her room.

"Serenity and Nightmare III, are you ready to go?" asks Dr. Clide.

Even now, Serenity looks like she could go back to bed.

"Yes, we are, Dr. Clide," says Nightmare III.

The doctor leads the way to his car by the fire escape that leads down to the employee parking lot. The three of them get into the car. Serenity lies down in the backseat of the car. Nightmare III and Dr. Clide sit in the front two seats, with Dr. Clide driving. Dr. Clide drives away from the hospital toward his home.

While on the highway, heading to Dr. Clide's house, the car suddenly goes off the road. Nobody is hurt, but now they are surrounded by enemies.

"Dr. Clide, please get her somewhere safe. I'll find you later," says Nightmare III as he jumps out of the car.

"Just be careful," says Dr. Clide, and then he drives off.

CHAPTER 25

Dr. Clide pulls into his driveway, arriving home a little after 10:00 p.m. Serenity is still asleep in the back seat of the car. Dr. Clide gets out of the car and walks to his house, opening the door to the house. Then he walks down the hall to the guest room and opens the door. He pulls the blankets down so that he could cover her after laying her down in bed. Dr. Clide then walks back out to the car, opens the back door, and picks up Serenity to carry her inside instead of waking her up. He lays her down on the bed and covers her up, then he walks to go shut the car and gets ready for bed himself. He wonders how someone could want to hurt a girl as beautiful and kind as Serenity.

The next morning, Dr. Clide goes to check on her and also to see if Nightmare III has arrived yet. He finds her still asleep in the guest room, but there is no sign of Nightmare III.

He goes into the kitchen to make breakfast, and as he is cooking, he looks over his shoulder to see Serenity in the doorway.

"Has Nightmare III shown up yet?" asks Serenity.

"No, he is not, Sweetheart. Stay calm. He'll show when it is safe enough to come to you," says Dr. Clide.

"I really need some type of blood supply," says Serenity.

"I've got plenty of blood bags in the refrigerator. Take what you need. My boss is letting me get as much as I need, knowing what you are and that it helps you get better quicker. He may stop by to check on your progress," says Dr. Clide.

"Okay, but I wish Nightmare III was here. I don't feel all that great alone, with no one I'm close to here," says Serenity.

"I'll take care of you. I'll do my best to keep you safe and comfortable as long as you're here," says Dr. Clide.

Serenity sits at the table, watching Dr. Clide cook breakfast. She doesn't know what to do, and she can't figure out why Nightmare III still has not shown up. Dr. Clide looks at her as if he wants to say something, but he stays quiet.

"Dr. Clide, why aren't you saying anything to me?" asks Serenity.
"It is not my place to judge Nightmare III's character," says Dr. Clide.
"Why not?" asks Serenity.
"Because I don't know him, and I'm not your father," says Dr. Clide.
Then Dr. Clide sets the table for two and joins her for breakfast.

CHAPTER 26

Serenity eats breakfast with Dr. Clide. Instead of showering, she turns on the TV, curious about what is happening outside the house.

She sees Nightmare's face on the screen and hears the words, "Found dead on side of the highway. We have no explanation as to why so many died, and there was no car at the scene— only tracks of a car . . ."

Serenity drops the remote control and screams. Her fear of hunters comes back a hundred times over. She starts to cry and then hears the TV reporter ask if anyone could come forward to identify the man in the photograph. The man is still alive but in critical condition.

Dr. Clide hears what the TV is saying and then turns to Serenity.

"I will take you to the hospital where Nightmare III is being treated, but you have to talk to the police first and tell them what you know," says Dr. Clide.

"I will," says Serenity in agreement.

Dr. Clide cleans up breakfast, while Serenity showers and puts on fresh pair of clothes. Dr. Clide and Serenity walk out of the house and get into his car. Dr. Clide drives Serenity to the hospital where Nightmare III is admitted. When they get to the hospital, Dr. Clide drops her off and heads to do his job at another hospital. Once Serenity enters the hospital, the cops ask for her photo identification card. She gives them her Russian ID, but they can't read it. She tells them her name in their language. They run it through the computer and nothing comes up except the fact she is not registered as a normal person but as a vampire.

"Can you speak English or Scottish?" asks the police officer.

"I was taught a few different languages, but I can understand what people are saying easily," Serenity tells the police in English.

"Okay, miss, tell us why you're here then," asks the police officer.

"You have a very close friend of mine here. I can tell you who he is and why you found so many people dead on side of the highway," says Serenity.

The police officer calls the nurse over.

"Is there a place where we can take a witness, and potentially a suspect, and have a talk?" asks the police officer.

All of a sudden, for the first time in her life, Serenity feels like she wants to flee authorities.

"Miss, are you all right?" asks the police officer.

She gives a weak smile.

"Miss, we just want to talk for now, nothing else," says the police officer.

"But why you would suspect me as the killer?" asks Serenity.

The police officer sidesteps the question.

"So you don't mind talking to us?" asks the police officer.

"No, because I know that I didn't do it," says Serenity.

"But do you know who did it?"

"Yes, but please let me explain things to you. It will all be clear then. But please don't harm that man in the bed over there. It's not his fault he's there and the others are dead," says Serenity.

"We'll see. Depending on what you tell us, miss," says the police officer.

CHAPTER 27

"This all started about three weeks ago when I arrived here by plane. I checked into a hotel right in town about thirty to forty minutes from here. I've been having trouble with a security team known as the Vampire Hunters—VHs, for short. It started back in America. I didn't think trouble would find me here," begins Serenity.

"This is entirely my fault. I had a fight with other VHs about a week after I arrived because they figured me out. They left me no choice. They threatened to blow up the hotel where I was staying," says Serenity.

She continues, "This last attack, Nightmare III caught them. Dr. Clide helped me escape because I was too weak to fight the VHs myself. Nightmare III wanted to protect me even if it cost him his life because he loves me more than I could ever explain. I'm very sorry for all the trouble I have caused the people here in Scotland."

"I really didn't mean to get anyone involved in my fight. I'll leave first thing in the morning on the next flight, so no one involved gets hurt. If you will excuse me, I would like to return to my hotel room to pack," explains Serenity.

"Hold on, missy. We are not mad at you. No matter where you go, you will get others involved in your fight. Let us try to help you first," says the police officer.

"I don't want anyone else hurt. This is my fight, and mine alone," says Serenity.

"It doesn't have to be that way if you let us help you," says the officer.

"But I don't want you guys to get hurt because of me," says Serenity.

"You don't worry about us. We can handle our own in a fight. You will only need to worry about yourself. Now go to your hotel, and two of our officers will meet you there and be watching you 24/7, seven days a week, as long as you are here," says the police officer.

"That is very kind, but I think it is best if I find another place to lay low. Could you do me a favor?" asks Serenity.

"What is it, miss? And please let us at least assist you until you catch your flight out of here," asks the police officer.

"Only if you protect Nightmare III until he leaves or at least until he is out of the hospital," says Serenity.

"Then you got yourself a deal, Ms. Serenity," says the police officer.

CHAPTER 28

Serenity is walking back to the hotel with two Scotland policemen. She stops at a shop and picks up a few necessary items for her trip.

"Are you really okay with leaving Nightmare III behind?" asks the police officer.

She looks up at them after thinking about it long and hard.

"No, but this is the best action I could take right now," says Serenity.

"Why is that, Ms. Serenity?" asks the police officer.

"I don't want anyone else hurt or involved with my fight," says Serenity.

"Serenity, you don't have to go into this fight alone. People want to help you," says the police officer.

"Yes, I do. You'll all die if you try to fight with vampire hunters," says Serenity.

"Serenity, why do you push everyone away?" asks the police officer.

"I do it because of what happened to Nightmare III," says Serenity.

"What happened to him?" inquires the police officer.

"What do you mean?" asks the police officer, not knowing the story.

"The nurse did not show you or have you not listened to the newscast on TV?" asks Serenity.

"No, I can't say that we have," says the police officer.

"What is it with people and their desire to fight a problem they don't understand, even when it could cost them their lives?" asks Serenity.

"We do it for the greater good," responds the police officer.

"Fine, but to be clear, I'm not going to be responsible for whatever may happen between now and the time I board my flight in the morning. Tonight may be the longest night you have ever known," says Serenity.

"We don't care. We are up for the challenge. We are willing to go to any lengths to keep you safe as long as you're in this country. We solemnly vow from now until you leave this great country, we will protect you at the cost of our very own lives," says the police officer.

"You two are really sweet. Now, let's get going," says Serenity.

They step out of the hospital and into the sunset. A mile down the road, twenty minutes from her hotel, they run into trouble. Several VHs surrounded them all at once from all directions.

"Missy, you have given us quite the chase," says one of the vampire hunters.

"No one runs from us this long and lives to talk about it. This ends right here," says a VH.

"I don't think so," says Serenity.

"Oh, come. Don't make us chase you to the ends of the Earth," says the VH.

"Why not? I'm not ready to die yet. You make me sick, knowing you will attack innocent vampires just to make your name known throughout VHS world."

Serenity is in a fight for her life with the VHs. She tells her company to take cover as she pricks her finger and exposes the blood-light whip, which will slice through anything in the way. When the policemen reemerge, all they see are the bodies of her enemies on the ground and the blood covering her hand.

"Serenity, was that really necessary?" asks the police officer.

"Yes, if I want to make it out of here alive," says Serenity.

"Why didn't you just injure them?" asks the police officer.

"If I did that, they would have still fought to the death. I showed them sympathy by killing them with one blow. Otherwise, it is just plain torture. So do you still want to stick around or part here?" asks Serenity.

"We are not going anywhere until you are aboard that plane and take off out of this country. Nothing you say or do will change our minds," says the police officer.

"Fine, but you guys are in for a reality check being with me," says Serenity.

Twenty minutes later, they show up at her hotel. She checks in, goes up to her room, and starts packing with Nightmare III on her mind. She starts to cry at the thought of leaving him behind. She sits at the desk, takes out the papers she brought with her, and starts to write a letter to him. When she is done, she licks the envelope and seals it shut so only he can read it, and she puts her seal on the back of it.

Twenty-Eight

Serenity didn't sleep at all the night before and goes to the airport early for her flight out to her new destination.

"You two, could I ask you to do a favor for me?" asks Serenity.

"What is it," ask the police officers.

"Could you take this letter to Nightmare after I leave?" asks Serenity.

"Sure, that will be easy if he is still at the hospital after you get on the plane," says one of the police officers.

"Thank you. That means a lot to me," says Serenity.

"Well, you better get going. They just did the final call for your flight," says one of the police officers

"I hope to see you next time I come to visit on better terms," says Serenity.

"Yes, that would be nice," says the officers.

Serenity walks up to the gate, gives her ticket to the attendant, and shows her passport. Then she boards the plane.

She looks out the window as the plane takes off and leaves Scotland where the love of her life and the nicest people and most accepting people she ever met are, but she should be moving on . . . for herself and everyone involved with her.

Serenity hears a horrific and terrifying sound as the plane soars high above the ocean. Water is a vampire's worse weakness on the planet. Serenity is only a few miles away from where she was born, a place she doesn't want to return to just yet. She needs to know that she is not being chased by vampire hunters anymore.

The pilots are not landing the plane because the air currents are strong. Serenity wants to get off this plane. She notices the plane starts to go down fast.

Serenity is in for the ride of her life. Vampires hate water. It is their mortal enemy if it has no herbal remedy qualities. The plane is heading straight for the ocean below.

She runs to the front of the airplane to take control and try to land safely on the ground. When she gets to the cockpit, she finds both the pilot and co-pilot shot dead. She takes the radio in her hand.

"Mayday, mayday," says Serenity over radio tower control.

After a few anxious minutes, she gets a response.

"I'm on a plane heading directly for the ocean," she tells the air traffic controller.

"Do you know how to fly a plane?" asks the air traffic control officer.

"No, how do I control it and where is the closest airport we can land on? We also have no pilots," says Serenity.

"Is it locked in autopilot?" asks the air traffic control officer.

"No, but I don't have any experience flying planes," says Serenity.

"Take the wheel and pull up. Try to get it straight out and ascend, then go left with it and keep it straight for three miles. Then slowly descend to the ground. After about four minutes, you will be able to see a runway. Land and head for the loading gate. Then stop the plane away from the gate, and the airport crew will take it from there," says air traffic control.

After Serenity manages to land the plane, she wants to run out of it like a bat out of hell. But she knows it's not the right thing to do even if the plane is filled with humans.

"Miss, the air marshal and the police would like to speak with you," says a flight attendant.

"Okay, lead me to them," says Serenity.

The flight attendant leads her off the plane while everyone else is ordered to remain seated. The police boards while waiting for the EMTs to arrive to check over the passengers.

CHAPTER 29

45

Serenity finds herself being questioned by the air marshals.

"We would like to test for gunpowder residue," says the air marshal.

Serenity agrees and also explains how she got blood on her hands.

"We want to see your identification card and passport to verify who you are," says the air marshal.

Serenity gives them both, nervous not because she's done anything wrong but because she needs blood and doesn't have any sources here since she is not allowed to touch federal agents. Serenity is getting light-headed and dizzy because it's been twelve hours since she last fed.

"Thank you for your cooperation. Your story checks out, Ms. Capulet. You're free to go," says one of the air marshals.

"Ms. Capulet, are you all right? Can we get you anything?" asks the air marshal.

"Only if you know where I can get free blood," says Serenity.

"Sure, come with us. We will get you set up with the hospital staff for an immediate blood transfusion. We may be back with more questions when you're better," says the air marshal.

CHAPTER 30

Nightmare wakes up to see a letter on the bed stand. He opens it carefully, noticing the royal seal on the envelope. He reads the letter.

Dear Nightmare,

I'm sorry to tell you this way, but under certain circumstances, I must go. I wish for you to follow your heart. If you want to find me and see me again, then go to the lands of the Capulets. If I make it through the trials ahead of me, I'll see you there in a few months.

I'm sorry, Love, for everything I put you through because of the Vampire Hunters Society. If I could change everything, you would not be involved in this fight of mine. The two things I regret are getting you involved in my fight and leaving you behind. I will never forget or regret the time we spent together. And the way you showed me how to really love another person . . . I hope fate brings you into my life again, and next time for life.

Sincerely,
Serenity Irshrose Capulet

Nightmare III begins to cry. The love of his life is gone and with it her beautiful, kind, loving smile. He realizes now, at this moment, that she is the love of his life, and fate has taken her away. Nightmare III takes the letter, treasuring it like it is all that is left of her here.

After spending a few more days in the hospital, he is released. A few hours later, he goes to the jewelry store and finds a ring Serenity will love. The ring is highly-priced, but he doesn't care. He will ask her to marry him the next time he sees her. He returns to his family's secondary castle.

In his room, he tries to get a grip on reality. In doing so, he realizes he needs to find her. When he does, he will tell her that whatever happened to him was not her fault and that she should not blame herself. Because what happened to him was what he got himself into because he loves her, and his love will never change for her one bit.

Nightmare is determined to be with the love of his life at any cost. After packing up his stuff, he goes to the airport to take the next flight to Russia. He can wait for Serenity to return home and hopefully meet her family when she gets home or before she gets there.

Nightmare waits patiently to catch his fight out of Scotland.

CHAPTER 31

Serenity leaves the hospital and walks around Spain, looking for a hotel where she can stay until the investigation of the dead pilots is over or until authorities say she is free to leave here and move on. Serenity is petrified that the VHS will find her here.

A male vampire spots her, which is not uncommon for Spain since many of her kind live here freely as long as they abide by the number one rule for vampires, which is not to drink from humans without their permission and never kill them.

"Miss, come here, please. I would like to talk to you," says the male vampire.

"Why, sir?" asks Serenity.

"Look at you, you're beautiful," says the male vampire.

"Back off, sir, I'm taken," says Serenity.

"Okay, miss, you leave me no choice," says the male vampire.

"What, do you want a fight?" asks Serenity.

"Yes, if I win, you come with me, and if you win, I leave you alone," says the male vampire.

"Fine. What type of fight are we talking about?" asks Serenity.

"A fight of no-touch magic. It's a fight where we use our magic to hit the other person, and the first one hit with magic by their opponent loses the game," explains the male vampire.

"Fine, if it will make you leave me alone in the end, I'll do it," says Serenity.

They head to the open field so that no bystanders get hurt and so that they can use their magic freely. After ten minutes of going back and forth with neither of them able to hit the other, Serenity finally gets him with strong magic, leaving a mark on him that he can feel burning him. She beats him fair and square.

"Sir, let me remove that magic. It is too strong for a fire user. I used too much of my spirit magic on you," says Serenity.

"Sorry, miss, for messing with you," says the male vampire.

Serenity can't stop thinking about Nightmare III back in Scotland. She can't stop thinking about the love they shared in his castle and bedroom.

After an hour of walking around, she finds a good hotel, and she makes it just in time. When she gets inside the hotel, it starts to downpour outside.

Serenity will spend the next few days there. It's safe, and it's raining too hard for her to go outside anyway. She doesn't know if she should laugh or cry because of her situation.

CHAPTER 32

Nightmare III wants to know Serenity's whereabouts.

"Excuse me. Have either of you ladies seen a woman with silver eyes, silver hair, and pale skin? She's dressed in a tank top with a v-cut most likely a dark color, black jeans, and black sneakers. She may have been wearing or carrying on a black trench coat," asks Nightmare III to off-duty flight attendants he came a cross heading to their next assignment.

"I heard about some trouble in Spain and that a young female passenger had to land a plane, saving everyone else on board. She fits the description you have given me," says one of the flight attendants.

"You wouldn't know when the next flight goes out to Spain?" asks Nightmare III in panic.

"Sir, we don't know but go over there, and the agent can tell you and book you out on the next flight to Spain," says one of the off-duty attendants.

"Thank you very much," says Nightmare III.

"You're welcome, and good luck finding her. She must be special if you're going to all this trouble to find her," says the flight attendant.

"She is the love of my life," says Nightmare III.

Nightmare walks over to the ticket booth to get a ticket out to Spain even though he just landed in Russia after flying from Scotland.

"Sir, can I help you?" asks the man at ticket booth for incoming and outgoing flights from Russia.

"Yes, I need to know when your next available flight out to Spain is," asks Nightmare III.

"Okay, here is your ticket, and the next flight is out shortly. You may want to head to the location for boarding your plane," says the man at the ticket booth.

Nightmare III's wait was very short, and he boards the plane anxiously to find Serenity. After the long flight from Russia, Nightmare III gets off the plane and collects his luggage. He goes out looking for a cheap hotel or motel to stay in under the radar until he finds Serenity—that is if she is still in Spain. He finds a cheap hotel that is not run down. Nightmare III walks into the office to get a room to stay in.

"I'm looking to get a room for a couple of nights," says Nightmare III.

"Okay, sir. Room 6 is open," says the man running the desk tonight.

"Thank you. I'll take it," says Nightmare III, paying in advance enough for a week.

Nightmare walks out of the office and down to Room 6, where he is staying. He walks inside his hotel room, exhausted and ready to crash after being up for two days straight. Nightmare III puts his "Do Not Disturb" sign on the outside of his door and then goes to bed. He starts to dream about Serenity and what they had and could still have.

When he wakes up, he unpacks, then goes out and begins his search. In the back of his mind, he knows he has a lot of ground to cover looking for Serenity.

After a while, he finds a nice restaurant to have lunch in. He orders food and eats it before heading back out to continue his search for Serenity. He goes to the center of Spain to see if she went to the most populated area to hide among the crowd. He searches all night but to no avail. So he goes back to his hotel to rest in hopes of finding her tomorrow night in a different part of Spain.

CHAPTER 33

It has been three days since Serenity landed in Spain. She goes down to the police station at the request of the air marshal and the detectives. Once inside, they bring her to an interrogation room.

"Ms. Serenity, would you need a drink or anything before we start?" asks the detective.

"Thanks, but no thank you," says Serenity.

"Okay, then I'll get right to the point of this meeting. I need a number to reach you at in case this goes to trial and we need you to testify on behalf of the people," says the detective.

Serenity gives them her phone number.

"Okay, you're free to leave Spain and go where you were heading. Here is your passport back. Have a good day, Ms. Serenity. Enjoy the rest of your stay here," says the detective.

Serenity wants to make sure she heard that correctly.

"So I can now leave Spain?" asks Serenity.

"Yes, you can, and please be safe doing so," says the detective.

"I will try my best but no guarantees," says Serenity.

Serenity leaves the police station and heads back to her hotel to pack up her stuff to head home. She can't keep her mind off how things used to be at home with a loving family and good friends. She looks forward to reuniting with everyone. Little does Serenity know her family is still not home yet and is still in separate parts of the world.

And little does she know at the airport where she will be landing in Russia not far from her homelands, the VHs are there, waiting for her to arrive to kidnap her.

CHAPTER 34

53·

Nightmare III starts searching the southern parts of Spain for Serenity. He wants his love back in his arms again. Little does he know that Serenity is preparing to catch a flight home.

He can't seem to get a grip on his emotions for Serenity. But he is not giving up on finding her, even if it is the last thing he does. Serenity is the only thing he wants to live for, even if it means fighting the VHs to the death to keep her safe.

But by the end of the night, he still isn't any closer to finding her. Nightmare III is starting to think she might have left Spain by now, but he doesn't know where she would go from here. He knows one thing for sure, and that is she's been the center of his world from when he first set eyes on her back in Scotland—where they first met on road leading to his family's second private castle home where his Grandfather Justin and Grandmother Lillian live out their days.

CHAPTER 35

Serenity lands in Russia after a nine-hour flight. She can tell hunters from the Vampire Hunter Society are already here. Serenity is still inside the airport, but the scent of a VH is unmistakable and can be picked up from a mile away, and she knows there are at least three in the airport.

She asks a ticketing agent when the next flight to China departs.

"In twenty minutes but it is booked. I can get you out on one at midnight tonight," says the agent.

"I'll take it then," says Serenity.

It is only 7:45 p.m., which means she has to avoid the VHs who are after her for the next four hours and twenty minutes. She checks her bags so that she doesn't have to carry them around.

She leaves the airport and goes to her favorite restaurant for a late dinner. She orders her favorite dish on the menu, which is a rare steak topped with mushrooms and cheese, with baked sweet potato topped with melted marshmallows. She also has a glass of strawberry lemonade made with fresh fruit.

After dinner, she heads back to the airport but suddenly realizes that she is being followed by the VHs. Serenity doesn't know what to do because she doesn't want to fight in a crowded street. So she leads them to an open field so that she doesn't have to worry too much about hurting innocent bystanders or attracting the attention of the authorities with the noise or the powers she needs to use to defeat the VHs.

She hopes that is the end of the VHs for now. Serenity is convinced that one of them was responsible for the deaths of the pilots as they try to kill her in a plane crash. She comes out of the fight without a scratch. She only has fresh blood on her fingertips from using the blood whip—one of the special abilities of high-ranking vampires more common in males than females. When Serenity is done with the vampire hunters, all that remains are ashes that are blown away in the wind. Serenity goes to a nearby stream to clean up before going back to the airport. She makes it back to the airport by 11:20 p.m., with ten minutes to spare before boarding time.

CHAPTER 36

Serenity is back on the plane, and her flight is going smoothly this time, at least for now. Serenity falls asleep with one thing on her mind and that is to keep the ones she loves at a safe distance until this fight is over.

She keeps having nightmares about what could happen and what still might happen to her family and Nightmare III. Serenity misses her family and her home so much. It is hard for Serenity to stay strong, but she is stronger than she even realizes. She is not a quitter even when odds are against her. But even now, there are times she feels like giving up and dying so that she doesn't have to live this nightmare that surrounds her all the time.

Little does she know that this is just the beginning of her nightmares, and things will get worse before they get better.

As she gets off the plane in China, she is almost immediately surrounded by the VHs. They lead her to their private jet and make her get on, knowing it is too crowded for her to fight them there.

On the plane, the VHs converse with each other, trying to figure out what to do with their prisoner when they land. The jet lands on a small island in the middle of nowhere. The only way in or out is by air or boat, but they only keep a jet on hand. Before they let her off the jet, they blindfold her to keep her disoriented. The vampire hunters lead her inland to one of their secret hideouts. After about two hours of walking, they get her into their hideout, which has no windows.

The VHs then lead her down a dark hallway lit by candlelight. After a few minutes, they suddenly stop. Serenity hears them talking and then suddenly feels someone shove her into a room and close the door behind them. She pulls off the blindfold. She is getting scared not knowing where she is and what they are planning to do with her. She is thinking they will use her in some twisted sick way like most people do to her kind since they can get away with it.

CHAPTER 37

It seems like hours have gone by since they put her in this empty room. Just when she thinks she won't see them again, a few VHs enter the room, throw another blindfold at her, and tell her to put it on. Serenity knows she is in no position to try to escape at the moment, so she goes along with their instructions. They walk her to another room where she is no longer alone, and they take off the blindfold.

This room is different. She can smell the deaths of fellow vampires in here. One of the vampire hunters who is very strong but too old to work the field is in this room. When she gets her vision focused, she realizes the man is taking off her clothes, slowly and carefully to tease her. She tries to scream but can't. After he has removed her clothes, the next thing she feels is his hands moving over her body.

She feels something go into her vagina and realizes his fingers are moving around in her and in and out, teasing her, toying with her. She is hoping it doesn't get any worse than this and violate her body. She hates what this VH is doing to her. She wants this torture to end. Little does she know that this is just the beginning.

He chained her to the bed, with her facing him. He gets undressed and gets on top of her, penetrating her as hard and violently as possible to cause her pain and suffering. She doesn't deserve this, but it is the way of the VHs who make vampires their mates.

After about an hour of this, she is returned to her room for the night, but there is still more to come. The VHs haven't gotten what they want out of her yet. She has become their puppet because she is a female vampire.

The Vampire Hunter Society has plans, and it is not for her to die. The plan is to attempt to get as many children from her as possible. The VHs want to make a baby machine out of her.

CHAPTER 38

Nightmare III books the next flight out to Russia, but he's stuck in Spain for another twelve hours. He hates the fact he doesn't know if she is safe or not. He hopes she is not in harm's way. Nightmare III doesn't want his beloved girl hurt, but he can't deny the fact that vampire hunters are after her.

"What do they want from her? Are they just out to kill her?" thinks Nightmare III, not knowing the answers.

Nightmare III would rather die protecting her than see her get hurt by others. He waits in agony and torture, not knowing what is going on with Serenity. Now, he has to wait a while more just to find out if she is even in Russia or if she has returned home yet. It is painful for Nightmare III to even consider that she actually might be in harm's way or even dead right now.

Once on the plane, Nightmare III falls asleep, but his sleep is actually a nightmare. In the dream, Serenity is running through the woods, being chased by VHs. They have guns of all sizes and shapes with special bullets that will paralyze or even kill a vampire if they hit in the right place.

They come to an open field, and Serenity doesn't have a chance to turn around and use the blood whip on her enemies. They shoot her dead center in the heart. She falls to the ground, bleeding in pain and screaming out. The shot alone does not kill her or paralyze her. It causes her agonizing pain. The hunters grab her and take her to a remote location, then chain her to a cross. The sun comes up over the mountain, and she starts to burn, but it isn't causing her to die. It just causes her more pain that she doesn't deserve just for what she is.

Nightmare III wakes up, shaking uncontrollably from his nightmare.

CHAPTER 39

Serenity wakes up to a bright light being turned on in her dark room. The VHs come in and grab her. They take her down to the same room as the day before, and she sees the same vampire hunter. She tries to get away but fails. She is shoved into the room, and the door closes behind her.

Serenity is trying to stay away from the VH in the room with her. She is scared he will do the same as he did the day before. Serenity doesn't want to be the VHs's pet. But she can't escape on her own. So she is trapped here for the time being. The man grabs her and pulls her down on the bed. She looks for exposed skin on his body. She finds an opening on his neck then bares her fangs and bites him really hard to puncture his skin, wanting to injure him badly. Serenity makes sure she doesn't put her venom in him, but she punctures one of his main veins. He stumbles and falls because of loss of blood. Some of his comrades and a doctor come in to treat his wound and restrain Serenity. They took her back to her room. The nurses and doctors repair the damage that Serenity did to the old vampire hunter. They had failed to take into account her fangs.

CHAPTER 40

The plane lands in Russia at noon the next day. Nightmare III is trying to find where Serenity would be or where her home is. He has no clue where her family lives. He starts walking the streets to find clues about her whereabouts. He sees a girl who looks similar, but she's not as pale-skinned as Serenity or as long-haired.

"Sir, are you okay? Are you lost?" asks a woman.

"I'm looking for someone. Have you seen her? Her name is Serenity," asks Nightmare III.

"Are you referring to young Princess Serenity Irshrose Capulet?" asks the woman.

"Yes, do you know where she is?" asks Nightmare III.

"I saw the VHS grab her and shove her onto a private jet, but I do not know where they went. Sorry, I can't be any more of a help in finding your friend," says the woman.

"It's fine. I'll find her and bring her back safely," says Nightmare III.

He knows it will be a race against time, and it is not in his favor either. The vampire hunters have a few days on him, at least. The VHs could be holding her anywhere in the world, in some place secluded and out of view—in a jungle, forest, or on an island in the middle of nowhere. He is worried about her safety with them.

PART 2

*Nightmare versus Cloud
for Serenity's Love*

CHAPTER 41

Serenity lies there, helpless and feeling sorry for herself because she was stupid not to take Nightmare III's help. She wishes that she just knew how to trust Nightmare III through this, but he is hiding something. And she was being an idiot thinking she could handle this herself and escape. Serenity wishes there was a way out of this hell hole that the VHS put her in.

Suddenly, she hears an uproar outside her room. She hears the VHs scrambling to try to fend someone off.

She walks toward the door, hearing the VHs smashing the ground. The door opens, and she sees not the VHs standing there but Cloud. She is shocked. It has been two weeks, and she didn't expect to see or hear from him again. He picks her up and starts to leave as more VHs arrive. Cloud covers Serenity's eyes, then uses harmless magic and knocks the VHs out. Finally, after a few minutes, he gets her out safely.

Outside of the VHs' hideout, he puts his hands around her tightly and takes off into the sky. Serenity is asleep in his arms miles above the ground. For the first time in a few days, she is finally getting sleep. Cloud looks down and thinks how lovely it is to see her safe and asleep in his arms. He realizes that he is in love with such a lovely creature. Cloud knows that she is a completely different creature from himself.

Cloud spots a cliff on the mountain below and leads on it. He then walks into the dark dreary cave with Serenity in his arms. Cloud is lucky that the cave is nice and deep and also about two hundred feet above the ground. Cloud doesn't know Serenity's limits or if she can be out in the daytime at all. Cloud plans on having Serenity stay here until nightfall for her own safety. He wraps his wings around them both to keep them protected. His wings are twenty feet long from tip to tip.

CHAPTER 42

It is early morning, and Nightmare III goes to order a boat ticket to an island where he thinks Serenity may be held captive. He wishes she would call him to let him know she is safe. The worst part is not knowing. He boards the ship and begins pacing to try to ease his mind. His heart is breaking from not being with Serenity.

When he calms down a bit, he sits down on the deck of the ship. He convinces himself that she is safe from harm right now. Nightmare III is watching the scenery pass by him. After about an hour he falls asleep, and he slips into another nightmare about Serenity.

In the middle of the night in the woods, he comes upon Serenity bleeding severely. He grabs her. Serenity's body is cold as ice—like she has been dead for quite some time. Serenity suddenly bites him and starts to drain him. He pulls away from her, terrified. She gets up and runs away, knowing that look that so many humans and demons alike have given her. Nightmare III chases after her, but after a while, he falls into a trap created by illusion—one of Serenity's specialties. He wakes up screaming, feeling still trapped in Serenity's illusions.

CHAPTER 43

It is dark outside when Serenity and Cloud get up and walk out on the cliff. Cloud watches Serenity closely on the cliff because she is not fully awake and could fall off. He knows how dangerous a half-asleep vampire can be when just waking up. Serenity's eyes are red from not feeding properly for at least two weeks. She could use a good feeder because she is really weak at the moment. Serenity and Cloud look at each other for a moment before Cloud grabs her and takes her into the sky without warning. After about twenty minutes of flying, Cloud spots a campsite. They don't have a choice but to check to see if humans or other demons are there, preferably humans.

When they land just outside the campsite, Cloud tucks his wings in tightly to his body to appear human so that he can blend in with the crowd. But the campsite is empty. All they find is food for humans. They eat some then take off, looking for humans or other demons that Serenity can feed off. He wants to get her home, but he wants her to be stable, not weak, when she gets there.

After about twenty miles, they spot what Serenity needs. They land away from the targets so that they don't scare the humans. Serenity and Cloud slowly approach. After they get close enough, all but one runs from Serenity's red eyes. Serenity takes the one who stayed and bites on the neck for blood. The boy doesn't fight her. After a minute of feeding, she puts the boy to sleep, erases his memory of her, and places him in the tent. She makes sure to heal her bite mark on his neck.

When Serenity closes the tent, Cloud grabs her and then takes her off into the sky with her in his arms. They are heading for her homeland. Cloud is happy that he has Serenity to himself. Serenity is watching everything that is going on around her. She loves the view but can't keep Nightmare III off her mind. Serenity won't look Cloud directly in the eyes. Cloud tilts her head up and kisses her on the lips. Serenity looks away, still distracted with Nightmare III on her mind.

They get to another cave just before dawn. The sun is dangerous for her fine pale skin. It could easily burn her.

CHAPTER 44

Nightmare III disembarks on the island, not far from where Cloud and Serenity have landed. Serenity sees Nightmare III and runs to him. He grabs her and spins her around in the air, happy as can be.

"Serenity are you okay?" asks Nightmare III.

"Yes, but I have a question for you, Nightmare III," says Serenity.

"What is it, Serenity dear?" asks Nightmare III.

"Were you the one who risked your life for me back on the battlefield in Scotland?" asks Serenity.

"That was me. Do you have something against me helping you?" asks Nightmare III.

"Of course not, but why did you do that, knowing you could have been killed by me or those hunters?" asks Serenity.

"Because I would have rather died protecting you than live without you?" says Nightmare III.

"I'm glad to see you again," says Serenity.

"Let me stay with you please, Serenity," asks Nightmare III.

"Will you follow me anyway if I said no?" asks Serenity.

"No, but I will worry about you," says Nightmare III.

"Okay, Nightmare III, I'll let you stay for now," says Serenity.

"Thank you, Serenity dear," says Nightmare III.

"You're welcome. We leave after nightfall," says Serenity.

In the cave, Nightmare III, Cloud, and Serenity decided to get sleep before they travel again. Cloud and Nightmare III both wake up an hour later. They are keeping guard to stay alert for danger. After a few hours, Nightmare III and Cloud leave the cave and go down to the ground to settle something between the two of them. They know it may hurt Serenity.

CHAPTER 45

Nightmare III and Cloud stand five feet apart in battle position, ready to fight one another. Nightmare III throws his cape to the side so that it doesn't get in the way. Cloud unfolds his wings. They draw their weapons. Cloud and Nightmare III are unaware that each can perform magic, but both are limited. After all, it is against falcon and vampire policy in the day world because it could affect it in dangerous ways. Falcons have their own land where they can practice and use all types of magic.

Cloud takes off into the sky, while Nightmare III uses his hands to control the magic to throw it at Cloud from the ground. Cloud dodges the attack and counters with his own magic, which is stronger than vampire magic. Nightmare III spots the magic ball and dodges it, then starts shooting magic and rapidly throwing any weapons he has on him. Cloud does the same, throwing magic along with weapons, but the weapons are also infused with magic for greater damage.

The fighting goes on for an hour before they finally run out of weapons, which are scattered all over the ground. Cloud's wings have been severely damaged in the fight, and from an aerial position, he falls thirty feet to the ground below. Nightmare III quickly grabs the closest sword and moves toward Cloud. Cloud gets up even though the fall has knocked the wind out of him, and he then grabs the closest sword to him. Nightmare III's sword is longer by an inch, but Cloud is highly trained and can counter any of Nightmare III's attacks.

Cloud started to mess with Nightmare III for the fun of it. Just killing him is no fun. Cloud wants Nightmare III to suffer. Cloud cuts up Nightmare III, bad enough to send the scent of blood up to the cave where Serenity is sleeping. Serenity wakes up to the smell of blood coming from below the cave. She rushes down, realizing both of them are missing from the cave. She is hoping she is not too late to stop the out-of-control fight between two demons fighting over who loves her more. Serenity hates seeing death even if it is unavoidable.

When she gets to the ground, she sees Cloud going for the killing blow. Serenity sends her own magic at Cloud to see if she can throw him off balance. She was successful, but only temporarily. Cloud regained his balance and starts rushing toward them. Cloud intends to kill Nightmare III to get Serenity to himself. But when he finally reaches them, he loses the heart to kill him in front of Serenity. So Cloud backs off and decides to wait for another time when Serenity is not around if that chance ever comes again. But the next time he tries, he won't toy with him so much.

After another hour of using her magic, Serenity is finally able to get Nightmare III in a stable state, but doing so causes her to pass out over using spirit magic. Cloud picks up all his weapons then grabs Serenity and takes her off into the sky, knowing it will be hours before Nightmare III will even be well enough to chase after them. Cloud is still planning to take Serenity to her homeland. He is hoping Serenity won't put up a fight when she finally comes to from the excessive use of her magic.

Serenity's body is covered in strange baby blue marks. The markings on her face look like face-painted tiger stripes. It starts above the eyes and goes down under the eyes, looking like z's and stripes. The marks go down toward the mouth and under it. The marks are weaved around her arms, legs, and neck. Her fingers look like they have ribbons on them. She even has blue stripes throughout her hair and a blue wing design on her back. All the blue on her body is from using her spirit magic. It is the most dangerous and forbidden magic in the vampire world. She is wearing a black tank top, jeans that fade from black to gray, and black sneakers.

CHAPTER 46

Nightmare III wakes up to find Serenity and Cloud gone. He doesn't understand why Serenity saved him again, or why she willingly left if that was the case. But Nightmare III has a feeling that she didn't leave here as willingly as he wants himself to believe. Nightmare III finds himself wondering if Serenity is even safe with Cloud. The one thing he does know is that he is no match against Cloud in a battle, for he lacks experience and training.

Nightmare III decides to find a blood source before going after Serenity. When he finds her, he will try to talk her out of seeing Cloud—someone he doesn't trust and whose motives he doesn't understand.

After about an hour of looking, he finds a campsite with humans in it. He casts a spell to make them fall asleep so that he can feed off them without them running away or being aware of his presence.

Nightmare III leaves the humans sleeping and goes after Serenity. He travels east toward Serenity's homeland, in hopes that is where they are going. Nightmare III can't stop thinking how stupid he was to leave Serenity alone with him and how stupid it was to go up against a falcon in vampire form. All Nightmare III wants now is for his love to be back by his side once again. Nightmare III knows she wants to go home for a bit before searching for her brother Scott. He wishes there was a way to beat the falcon at his own game.

CHAPTER 47

They slept all day in the cave. Serenity wakes up early and leaves the cave. She is now traveling home alone. Twenty minutes later, she comes across the campsite. Serenity finds seven people, all of them staring at her. She casts a simple spell that knocks them out. She feeds off them and puts them to bed and leaves to head home. Serenity is thinking about how much she doesn't want Cloud near her or Nightmare III right now.

Serenity keeps walking, wanting to get home to find out if anyone from her family is home yet. Little does she know her family is safe but not home because they are sticking to the plan they made back in America. Her younger brother is still in Japan. Her mother Janine and her father Jonathan are still in China. Serenity wishes she knew how her family is doing and when she can see them again, but she can't call them. It hurts Serenity to be away from her family. It's been two months since she has seen anyone from her family.

A few hours have passed since she left Cloud. It is getting lights out, and Serenity finds a hiding spot among the standing trees. Her breathing becomes shallow and quiet so that she can't be heard. Serenity doesn't want to be found by Cloud. She's had enough of him. Cloud is not her love, and she has had enough of Nightmare III too. She is not sure who she wants to love. So Serenity waits and rests. Since it is close to sunrise, she plans to wait until the night before leaving to head home.

CHAPTER 48

Cloud wakes up, realizing he slept all night and that Serenity didn't even bother to wake him up. He knows she is traveling alone now and that Nightmare III probably hasn't caught up to her yet. Cloud hopes she doesn't know how to conceal herself from everyone. He can recognize Serenity's feeding pattern as he searches for her. He hopes she didn't get too far from where she last fed. He knows his chances of finding her in the daytime are slim, but he has to try. Trying to find Serenity in the daytime is like trying to find a needle in a haystack.

He Is looking for her from the sky. He flies over her without even knowing it because she is well hidden among the trees, and magic has been concealing her presence. He finally gives up. After a full day of looking for Serenity, he crashes to the ground, passing out.

Serenity wakes up, sensing it is nightfall. She picks up Cloud's scent and climbs to the top of the tree to see where the scent is coming from and how she can get past him without being spotted. Serenity is an expert tree jumper. She has been jumping trees since she was a little girl. She uses her tree-jumping skills now so that she doesn't make too much of a sound. She doesn't want to get caught by Cloud.

CHAPTER 49

After a few hours, Serenity makes it off the island. She starts to run on water to get to the next closest country or island. Serenity wants to get far away from Cloud and closer to home. Serenity spots a boat and gets on it, then finds her way to an open room, hoping she doesn't get caught by the captain. She realizes she's in a room with no windows, which is fine with her since she can't stand the sun and doesn't want the sunlight coming in while she is resting. Being on a boat is the last place Cloud would think she would escape to since vampires hate water. Now he can keep guessing where she is or if she is still on the same island as him.

Serenity wakes up hungry and hears people screaming for help. She spots people trapped. She finds a layout of the ship and memorizes it, and now all she has to do is get the passengers to follow her to safety. It takes her a few minutes to get the people to calm down and listen to her. Serenity tells them there is another way to get to the deck and that if they follow her, they can make it out safely. Everyone follows her lead to the back of the stairwell and up to the deck, where the captain is doing a head count of everyone on board.

Serenity stays, even though she knows she will have to explain herself to the captain. The captain walks up to her.

"Miss, what is your name? You're not on the roster," inquires the captain.

"My name is Serenity Irshrose Capulet," answers Serenity.

"Why and how did you get on board?" asks the captain.

"I need a place to hide from someone, so I sneak on board from the back of the ship," says Serenity.

"While you are on my ship, you will go by my orders and my crew's orders. You will stay with everyone on the ship until we reach land, and then you can do what you want when everyone is safe," Captain Jackson instructs.

"Yes, Captain, understood," says Serenity.

All the women and children, including Serenity, get into the emergency lifeboats first. The crew then prepares them to be lowered down into the water. Serenity and twenty others are lowered down first. Serenity sits and watches as other boats are lowered down. She can't help but think that she is partly responsible for the trouble on the boat and that if she wasn't on it, everyone would be fine.

It is close to dawn. She is getting tired and restless because her fine skin is so sensitive to light. A woman with a long coat puts it on Serenity and pulls the hood over her head. Serenity falls asleep against the woman, too tired to stay awake. Everyone has to take turns rowing the boat, but they all let Serenity sleep and stay fully covered. Every passenger on the rowboat with Serenity can tell that she's not doing well with the sunup.

After about two hours, a ship spots the lifeboats and pulls up next to them, preparing to take the weary survivors to the next port. The captain of the abandoned ship asks if there is a way to get one of his passengers on board without waking her up or exposing her sensitive skin.

"Yes, but she will have to be taken up first," says the first mate of the rescue ship.

He throws a blanket down to the lifeboat so that the passengers can wrap her up before he goes down to grab her. He picks up Serenity and rests her across his chest. One of his arms is under her legs, supporting her, and the other one is holding onto the railing.

After he gets Serenity and himself on board, the first mate takes her to a safe room where she can sleep in.

Back up on deck, the two captains start to talk about what happened on the other ship. They conclude that someone is targeting the young girl who is asleep, but they don't know why because she is a kind person and has saved the lives of many passengers. Captain Mason offered to take Serenity to her homeland for free. Captain Jackson takes him up on his offer, knowing Captain Mason's ship won't be taken by surprise or be taken down easily.

He also knows that Captain Mason's current destination is Russia, but they are stopping at a station at the halfway point to drop off Captain Jackson, his crew, and the passengers to get relocated to a ship to continue on their journey.

Serenity wakes up, and the man who helped her out of the lifeboat walks into the room.

"Ms. Serenity, is everything okay?" he asks.

"Why did we stop?" asks Serenity.

"We're dropping off Captain Jackson, his crew, and the passengers. My captain wants you to stay on board with us," says the first mate.

"Why does he want me to stay? All I want to do is go home to my family's land and meet up with them. I miss them very much," says Serenity.

"My captain is going to Russia. That is why he wants you to stay with us," says the first mate.

Reassured, Serenity falls right back to sleep. It is still daytime, and she needs her rest.

CHAPTER 50

Cloud has been flying for hours, looking for Serenity, but he finds Nightmare III instead. He lands to challenge him to another fight for Serenity's love. But they both know each other's abilities, so it will be more difficult for either of them to win this time. Cloud flies back into the sky, thinking it will give him an advantage over Nightmare III. Cloud and Nightmare III keep throwing magic at each other. Nightmare III keeps dodging Cloud's attacks. Because of the wind factor, Cloud is having a difficult time dodging Nightmare III's attack on him. So Cloud returns to the ground and grabs the sword he has been carrying with him on his back to defend himself against Nightmare III.

Nightmare III and Cloud take a fighting stance, facing each other out of respect for one another. They start with swords crossing in an X shape. Cloud and Nightmare III are fighting to find out who is the better man, but both men are completely blind to the fact that Serenity already escaped off the island and is heading home on a ship full of blood supplies. But she only takes what she needs, and she does not kill her prey. Nightmare III and Cloud are about evenly matched at sword fighting. Both are beaten up badly and have severe wounds on their shoulders and sides.

The two fighters collapsed from exhaustion and blood loss. A group of campers finds them about two hours later. The campers check to see if they have a pulse. Cloud has a very faint pulse, and Nightmare III has a stronger one but not as strong as his will to survive. The campers call 911 for an emergency. EMTs arrive twenty minutes later, and they recheck their pulses. Cloud's pulse is non-existent to humans. Nightmare III still has a faint pulse, barely alive. The EMTs rush Nightmare III to the hospital to get him into emergency surgery, hopefully to save his life.

CHAPTER 51

Serenity wakes up as the ship docks in Russia's port. She speaks with Captain Mason before she gets off, knowing she may not be staying home very long. She needs to find out if anyone has returned home to know who she still has to go and bring home and if anyone broke the plan they made back in America. Serenity walks up to Captain Mason, seeing him on the deck where everyone is disembarking.

"How long are you staying here in the Russian port, and where are you heading next?" asks Serenity.

"My ship is due to leave in two days, and our destination is Japan. Is there anything I can do for you, Princess?" asks Captain Mason.

"Yes, you can. If I'm back in time, could you take me with you to Japan?" asks Serenity.

"It would be my pleasure to assist you, Princess Serenity," says Captain Mason.

"Thank you, Captain Mason," says Serenity.

Serenity leaves the ship and walks until she is away from the crowd. She whistles, calling her horse to her. A white mare named Icicle comes galloping up to her master. Icicle is a pure white horse with black eyes. Serenity gets on Icicle and rides off to her home, which would have been a four-hour walk if it wasn't for Icicle coming to her aid. She really needs to know if anyone has returned home yet, even though the chances are very slim. Serenity hopes that they may be there, waiting for her to return.

After two hours of riding horseback, she makes it home to her family castle. When she enters the castle, her servants come up to her, shocked to see her home so soon.

"Princess, you have returned home earlier than expected," says the head servant.

"Yes, I have but have my parents or younger brother returned home yet?" inquires Serenity.

"Sorry, Princess Serenity, but they have not," says her head servant.

"It is all right. I need you to wake me up at nightfall and have dinner and a feeder ready for me. I need to pack and leave here at midnight to meet up with a friend. I will leave and head to Japan to find my young brother Scott," says Serenity.

"Would you like me to prepare your bath for you so that you can bathe before your journey?" asks the head servant.

"Yes, please, and don't worry about my clothes. I'll get those out later. And thank you," says Serenity.

When the servant leaves her room, Serenity sits down to brush her hair, but she starts crying once it hits her that she is the only one at home. Her mother won't be here to help her with the snarls and spend time with her. She is very close to her mother. Serenity remembers what it was like and how her mother always treated her like she is the land's most secret and treasured jewel.

One of the servants comes in. She picks up Serenity's hairbrush and starts to brush her hair out for her.

"Princess Serenity, why are you crying? No one has ever seen you cry before," asks Roza.

"I miss my mom. She always helps me whenever I get frustrated with my hair, trying to brush it out," confesses Serenity.

"Princess, you know I'll always be here for you. We grew up together and played together as children," says Roza.

"How can I forget that, Roza? I always got you in trouble with my father, and then I hid in my room until my mother comes home and finds me crying," says Serenity.

"You were happy playing with me inside the castle when your brother wanted you to go out in the daylight, but you never liked going outside when it was sunny out," says Roza.

"I know, Roza. I really never wanted to go out until nightfall, but there were times I had to and then I hid myself in the shadows and fell asleep until someone found us or night had fallen upon the earth," says Serenity.

"Yes, Princess Serenity, those were good days," says Roza.

Roza finishes brushing Serenity's hair and goes to leave the room.

"Roza, please stay with me for a while," asks Serenity.

"Yes, my princess, anything for you," says Roza, happy to stay with her old friend for a while.

Roza stays with Serenity until she is sound asleep. Then Roza goes to do some preparations for when her friend, the princess, wakes up and leaves again so soon. Roza wishes her princess could stay longer but knows whatever the princess is planning on doing must be important, or she wouldn't be parting again so suddenly.

CHAPTER 52

Nightmare III leaves the hospital to go find Serenity. From the information he was given by the doctors, the man he was fighting died at the scene. Nightmare III doubts that the falcon is truly dead. Little does he know that Serenity has already made it home and is now planning to head out to Japan shortly to go find her young brother. He is heading to Russia to find Serenity.

Nightmare III goes to the beach on the island to see if there is a ship ready to depart. He approaches the ship and walks up to the captain.

"Can I please come aboard your ship," asks Nightmare III.

"Where are you traveling to?" asks the captain. "I am heading to Russia, but it is a five-day trip from here."

"That is fine with me," says Nightmare III.

"Then welcome aboard," says the captain.

He gets a room and goes to bed to get some sleep since he was up most of the day, looking for a way off the island. Like vampires, dragons need some blood but not as often as vampires. The captain knows the risk of having a demon on board the ship if the passengers find out about him.

CHAPTER 53

Roza enters Serenity's room, then goes into Serenity's private bathroom to get the water ready for her friend, Princess Serenity. Roza knows Princess Serenity will go for the bath first after she wakes her up from her rest. Roza tends to whatever Princess Serenity needs, while the other servants prepare and cook Princess Serenity's meal.

"Princess Serenity, it is time to get up and get ready for your trip," says Roza.

"Is my bath prepared for me the way I like it?" asks Serenity, still sleepy after just waking up.

"Yes, Princess Serenity, along with your bath towel and favorite bathrobe," says Roza.

"Thank you, Roza. And please, no more calling me princess when we're alone. We've been friends since we were kids. My title shouldn't separate that," says Serenity.

"Yes, Prin—Serenity. I understand," says Roza.

Serenity goes into the bathroom and undresses to get into a relaxing bath before she has to leave again to go after her younger brother. It is only 4:00 p.m., but she still has a lot to do plus a two-hour horseback ride back to the port. The sun doesn't set until 6:00 p.m. anyway. Serenity has plenty of time to bathe, eat, pack, and get back to the port for her long journey to search for her younger brother. Then after she finds him and makes sure he is home safely, she will go after her parents who she misses the most right now.

After a half hour of relaxing and cleaning her body and washing her hair, she dries off, puts her silk bathrobe on, and goes back into her bedroom. She dries her hair off with her towel and then goes to find something to wear back to the ship.

Serenity puts on a dress that goes above her knees. It is a baby blue dress that fades to white at the sleeves. She puts on a few armor pieces that came with it. It is short in the front and goes longer in the back. It is fancy but would be considered middle-class clothing. She is going for the look that doesn't scream royal, but if anyone checks her passport or ID it will have her family's royal symbol on it of Russia. The symbol can either allow her to get what she needs or get her killed by her father's enemies. But Serenity is not the type to take advantage of her family's power or misuse her royal name. Serenity got her looks and powers from her father, but her fighting abilities from her mother. She has rarely had to use them. She developed some of her own fighting abilities too.

After packing, Serenity goes to get some food and a feeder before leaving to keep up her strength before meeting up with Captain Mason and his crew. Serenity notices on her way to the dining hall for dinner that one of her wolves is missing. He is her favorite wolf and also the most dangerous one to have.

When she calls him, Duke comes to her, recognizing her voice and knowing that he is in trouble now that his master is home. He follows her back to his pen. She is the only one he listens to. It is now ten minutes before seven, and Serenity makes it to the dining hall to get some dinner, which will be served as soon as she takes her seat.

She eats everything she wants. As she leaves the dining hall, she is met by Roza, who gives her a bag. Serenity leaves without saying a word to Roza, not wanting her to know that she is very sad. Serenity already takes off on Icicle for the port, even though she knows she will be a few hours early. Serenity knows Captain Mason won't mind or care and will be happy to see her and thinks of her as a companion for another trip out to the sea.

CHAPTER 54

A group of falcons spot Cloud from the air and swoops down, gathering around his body and returning to human form. They look to see if they can treat him or do anything for him. When they check his pulse, he is surprisingly still alive, but the falcons know that any normal human wouldn't be able to tell if he is still alive or really dead. The leader of the group, General Alex, tells the other members that they need to use their magic as a group to save the man's life. So they gather around in a circle, with General Alex standing at Cloud's head. They start saying a chant to heal his wounds and any internal damage done by the sword fight. The chant is in an ancient lost language that no one but falcons and some rare types of demons can understand.

After an hour, Cloud pulls through, and his stomach starts to rumble.

"General Alex, why are you out here, sir?" asks Cloud, alarmed that he may be in trouble.

"Because I heard a report that you were fighting a vampire," says General Alex.

"I did. It came down to a draw, but I don't know what happened to him, and I'm not sure if he is a real vampire. I believe that he may be some kind of shifter," says Cloud.

"It is fine if he is still alive for now," says General Alex.

"But, sir, he knows about us," says Cloud.

"Cloud, drop this now. It is a direct order. We can deal with him later if it comes down to him telling anyone. Do I make myself clear?" asks General Alex.

"Yes, sir. Understood, sir," says Cloud.

General Alex, Cloud, and the rest of the group head for Serenity's homeland to find her, hopefully before Nightmare III does.

CHAPTER 55

Serenity has been traveling for two hours now on horseback, and she finally sees the port. She dismounts Icicle and walks the rest of the way. It is too dangerous to have Icicle any closer to the ports in Russia. They aren't animal friendly there.

She goes to Captain Mason's ship right away, even though it will be hours before they set sail out to Japan. The passengers reload at 7:00 a.m. It's about 1:00 a.m. when Serenity is able to find Captain Mason and get aboard first.

"Princess Serenity, you were able to make it this lovely early morning," says Captain Mason, greeting her.

"Yes, it is. Could I please join you for another trip?" asks Serenity.

"Most certainly, Princess Serenity. I would be honored to have you aboard my cruise ship once again," says Captain Mason.

Little does Serenity know that Captain Mason likes her more than he is letting on.

Serenity picks the room she wants, but she doesn't realize that it is right across from the captain's quarters this time. She prepares for the week-long journey to Japan. She picks up her locket and opens it to see a picture of her brothers on one side and her parents on the other side. It was given to her by her mother the year before on her birthday. The locket is in the shape of a silver heart, and she keeps it with her at all times unless she knows she doesn't want it broken in a fight.

EPILOGUE

Nightmare III is halfway to Russia on a ship when he hears someone or something lands on the ship. It is around midnight, so he goes to the deck to find out what's going on. He recognizes Cloud right off, even though he is converting from bird form to human form.

"Cloud, what are you doing here? I thought I killed you back on the island," says Nightmare III.

"I could ask you the same thing since we came to a draw," says Cloud.

"I guess we are both lucky and stronger than we gave each other credit for since we don't know anything about each other," says Nightmare III.

"I'll agree to that. I also have a proposal for you, Nightmare III, even though we hate each other," says Cloud.

"Okay, let's hear it," says Nightmare III.

"We work together to find Serenity and help her with whatever she is trying to accomplish on her own," says Cloud.

"Fine, but it doesn't mean we're friends know, Cloud," says Nightmare III.

"I know, but Serenity could use all the help we can give her while fighting her enemies, even if it means she loves one of us more than the other one," says Cloud.

"So where should she head now?" asks Nightmare III.

"We should start at her home in Russia to find out if she had been home or if they know where she is heading. Then we'll take it from there," says Cloud.

"That sounds good, but we should stay on the ship for now. We both could use some rest, plus we're still too far from any island to fly. And Serenity can't travel by day anyway if she is walking," says Nightmare III.

They rest up until everyone else goes to bed, then they head to the deck, and Cloud takes off into the sky to see if Nightmare III knows how to fly. When Nightmare III doesn't spread his wings and take off after him, Cloud swoops down and grabs him to carry him to Russia. At the moment, Cloud has the advantage over Nightmare III and could drop him to his death. Nightmare III doesn't plan to make Cloud angry at him until they find out if Serenity is safe from harm.

After several hours of flying, they make it to an island. There, they find a cave to rest in for a few hours before making the final three-hour flight to Russia. They sleep until nightfall so that Cloud can regain his strength to carry Nightmare III again.

The only thing Nightmare III knows about Serenity's home is that her family is wealthy. He doesn't even know what her home looks like. He is soon going to find out the truth about her family, which he is not prepared for.

Cloud and Nightmare III take off in silence. Cloud flies gracefully even though he is carrying another male who is supposedly a vampire and weighs as much as he does. They've been flying for three hours when they hear a shot from below. Cloud looks down and recognizes the Capulet symbol on the flags hanging on the top of the castle where the guards are shooting from.

When they approach the castle's front gates, two of the guards get in their way.

"What brings you here, especially you, Cloud? You know better to come here unannounced," says Charles Grincory.

Charles is also known as Serenity's private head general.

"I'm sorry, but we need to know where Princess Serenity is," says Cloud.

"I don't personally know where Serenity went to, but I can take you to someone who would, so please come in, Cloud, and bring your friend," says Charles Grincory.

"Okay, lead the way," says Cloud, grinning to not show anger about Charles referring to Nightmare III as his friend.

It is beneath him to consider Nightmare III anything but an enemy.

Cloud, Nightmare III, and Charles walk in silence through the hallways that neither Cloud nor Nightmare III had been in before. Cloud has never been this deep in the castle, and Nightmare III has never been in the castle before. They study the hallways in case they have to show themselves out later.

They come upon a servant of Serenity.

"Roza, Cloud here needs to talk to you if you're not busy right now," says Charles.

"I've got some free time right now, Charles, sir," says Roza.

Roza turns her attention to Cloud.

"Cloud, how can I be of help you tonight?" asks Roza

"Do you know where Princess Serenity is and how I can find her? And how do you know who I am when Charles didn't point me out?" asks Cloud.

"She is heading for Japan to find her younger brother. Princess Serenity and I have seen you here before. Plus, she has shown me a picture of you and her as kids," says Roza

"Thanks, we must be leaving to find her now," says Cloud.

"Not so fast, you two. The sun is almost up, and I can tell you need rest, especially you, Cloud," says Charles.

Charles turns to Roza before speaking.

"Roza, prepare them a room to stay in," says Charles.

Roza leaves to get their room ready. All Roza can think about is how it has been a week since Serenity left here. But it is one thing she is not willing to tell them straight out. Roza has no desire to tell them how long it has been since Serenity left. Cloud and Nightmare III go to bed knowing Serenity has put some distance between them but not sure how much.

They sleep peacefully even though Serenity is so far away. It is because of the fragrance Roza put in the room to make sure they get enough sleep before going and helping Serenity. Serenity is Roza's best friend and princess.

Cloud and Nightmare III wake up at the same time. They are preparing to leave soon, hopefully to get to Serenity before she gets to Japan. Cloud and Nightmare III want to help Serenity and protect her so badly. After about an hour of preparing and getting dinner, they finally take off together to find Serenity.